goat days

THE INDIA LIST

goat days

BENYAMIN

Translated by
Joseph Koyippally

LONDON NEW YORK CALCUTTA

SERIES EDITOR
Arunava Sinha

Seagull Books, 2016

First Published in India in 2012 by Penguin Books India
Original © Benyamin, 2012
English translation © Joseph Koyipally, 2012

Printed in arrangement with Penguin Books India.
This edition is not for sale in the Indian subcontinent (India, Pakistan,
Sri Lanka, Bangladesh, Nepal, Bhutan, Myanmar and the Maldives),
Singapore, Malaysia and the UAE.

ISBN 978 0 8574 2 395 5

British Library Cataloguing-in-Publication Data
A catalogue record for this book is available from the British Library.

Typeset in Sabon by Eleven Arts, Delhi, India
Printed and bound by Hyam Enterprises, Calcutta, India

Prison

||||

One

Like two defeated men, Hameed and I stood for a while in front of the small police station at Batha. Two policemen were sitting in the sentry box near the gate. One was reading something. His posture, the way he moved his head, and his half-closed eyes, suggested that it was a religious text. The second policeman was on the telephone. His laughter and chatter audible in the street. Although the two sat close to each other, they were in different worlds. Neither worlds cared for us.

Slightly off the sentry box, a wild lemon tree curved into the street. We squatted in its shade, hoping a guard would look up from his work and notice us. We remained like that for a long time. Meanwhile, one or two Arabs briskly went into the police station and at least three or four sauntered out. It was as if we were invisible to them. Then a police vehicle came out of the station compound. We jumped up, eagerly following it with our eyes. But, stopping only to watch for vehicles on either side of the main street, it went its way. Feeling desperate, we leaned against the tree.

Whenever we thought the guard on the phone had ended his call, we would anxiously rise and walk up to the sentry box. It was futile though, for he would make another call without losing even a moment. The other sentry was so immersed in his reading that there was no sign he would look up any time soon.

We even walked past the sentry box a couple of times just to draw their attention. However, they did not notice us.

Haven't we all heard about so many unfortunate people who, for some emergency, left their rooms without the *pathaka* and got arrested in the market, in public places or in front of mosques. How many days did we walk through the vegetable market, the fish market and busy streets hoping to get arrested? Many a *muthawwa* went past us, not one stopped us. Many a policeman came across us, none checked us. What's more, we even loitered near mosques during prayer times without going in to pray. We tried it at several mosques and during different parts of the day. Still no one noticed us. One day, I even deliberately tripped on a policeman's foot. Instead of questioning me, he lifted me up, apologized profusely in the name of Allah and sent me away. Why is it that even misfortune hesitates to visit us when we need it desperately?

Finally, seeing no other way, we chose to come and stand in front of the police station; still, no use. After a while, we decided to cross the sentries and walk into the station. As soon as the suggestion came from Hameed, I got up and started walking, as if I had been waiting to hear it. I couldn't wait any longer. As we went past the long iron crossbar, the sentry who was reading raised his eyes and called us. We went back to the sentry box and said we wanted to see the *mudeer*. Gesturing us to proceed, he went back to his book.

We stepped into the police station and climbed up a long flight of steps, walking past doors bearing large inscriptions of verses from the Quran. Under a notice board in which papers were pinned like decoration, we spotted some policemen sitting and eating *khubus* and drinking *kahwa*, talking noisily. We stood quietly in front of the counter. On seeing us, one of them broke away from the conversation and raised his eyebrows while he continued to eat.

I gestured with my hand to show that I didn't know the language. Another policeman, with a kahwa cup in his hand, rose from his seat, came towards us and asked us for our pathakas. Yes, finally, someone asked the question! We helplessly shook our heads to say we didn't have it. He placed the kahwa cup on the table, opened the drawer, took a tissue paper and wiped his hands and lips. Then walking inside, he signalled us to follow him.

He took us to the room of the mudeer who looked up from the computer screen when he saw us enter. The policeman who escorted us told the mudeer something and he asked us something. We didn't betray any signs of understanding. I did not have to pretend; I really didn't understand most of what the policeman said or what the mudeer asked. But Hameed had to put on an act. I had heard him speaking fluent Arabic. Again, the mudeer and the policeman talked about something. Meanwhile, I scanned his room. It was a large office. On the walls were verses from the Quran, portraits of kings and a picture of the Kaaba. On the left from where the mudeer was sitting was a TV and on his right, a computer. A little further away, a sofa and a teapoy. On the teapoy was a flower vase with some plastic flowers. The wall opposite had a board with some photos pinned on it. I gazed at those photos. Bearded people with dead-fish eyes, Blacks in Arab dress. The Arabic lettering beneath each must have been their names. When I reached the third photo in the fourth row, my eyes froze like polar ice. I shook my head and looked at it again carefully. My heart began to pound and a sudden panic gripped me. Without realizing what I was doing, I began to walk towards the board on which the photo was stuck. Ibrahim Khadiri! I placed my hand on my heart.

'What? Do you know him?' the policeman asked me. I felt panic-stricken. The change in my manner was obvious. Still, I shook my head in a no. The mudeer called me and when I went up to him, he jumped up and slapped me across my ear. Oh! Only I remember how pain steamed out through the other ear. 'If you don't know him, why did you go to look at the photo?' the mudeer bellowed. I stood with my head bowed. He asked me something else in Arabic. I didn't answer. Finally, after cracking another slap, he sank back into his chair. I didn't cry. But Hameed did, so he didn't get slapped. The mudeer gave the policeman some instructions. We were taken to another room and handed over to another policeman. He opened a cabinet, took out handcuffs and put them on us, after which he made us sit on a bench.

Like us, the four or five others there were also in
handcuffs. I doubt if any of them were as happy to be
arrested as we were. In the afternoon, the cuffs were
removed and we were put in a cell. Six people occupied
the cell that could hardly accommodate three. I recall
a Malayali named Kumar among them. He had been
working in a vegetable shop and was arrested because
his Arab had accused him of theft. As for the two
Arabs and the Pakistani in our cell, I don't know what
crimes they had been charged with.

None of us could sleep that night, as we sat
packed together like we were in an overcrowded train
compartment. And with the Arabs spreading their
legs comfortably, others had to suffer even more.
Still, compared to what I had endured, that narrow
cell was heaven to me.

The next morning, after tea, we were handcuffed
again and taken out in a vehicle. There were other
handcuffed people in that vehicle who tried to
get acquainted with one another. Even among
them, Hameed and I remained silent and kept our
heads bowed.

After a long journey, the vehicle stopped inside
the compound of the largest prison in the country,
Sumesi. Many vehicles from different corners of the

country entered the prison yard at various times; from each, hundreds of 'criminals' came out. Absurd as it sounds, this scene reminded me of the marriage halls back home—the prisoners resembled the groom's tired relatives milling about the venue. Now I had become one such relative!

Once out of the vehicle, we were taken to the warden's office. It was very busy there. Many policemen came and went. Lawyers came and went. Muthawwas came and went. Arabs, too, came and went. At a glance, it reminded me of the porticos of our courts. There was quite a long queue in front of the warden's office and we took our place at the end. The policemen who came with us sat down in the shade of the veranda, a short distance away from the queue. We inched ahead as each person was called inside. I knew that the line was slowly taking us into the prison, and I was anxious about what awaited me inside. But I was also quite excited, almost like someone standing in front of the polling station to cast one's ballot for the first time. Slyly, I muttered my thoughts to Hameed.

We crept forward, and finally I was at the head of the queue. In the three minutes of waiting that followed, I felt a disquiet I find difficult to explain.

I was called, and the policeman who had come with us also rose and followed me in. The warden had a register in front of him. Based on the paper the policeman handed over and some details he supplied, something was noted in the register. Then I was made to sign in the column at the left end of the page. After that I was led to another policeman who tattooed some Arabic letters on my forearm with some kind of ink. I had been to a madrassa as a child, so I knew enough to identify it as the number 13858. Maybe the only use I ever made of the madrassa education.

The hall I entered was an interesting place. Barbers sat in a line from one end to the other. The policeman at the door sent me to a barber who had just finished with another person. These men worked at unimaginable speed. One could only feel the movement of the trimmer on one's head. It took them two minutes—at the most, three—to complete the job perfectly.

As I sat in front of the barber with my head bowed, I got a peep of Hameed sitting in front of the barber next to mine. We were done almost at the same time. I looked at Hameed's face, and he at mine. Two baldies. We laughed. A rare moment of mirth in times of great sorrow!

We were then taken to the large prison building. It was larger than what is normally considered a large building. It was colossal, spread over two or three kilometres and separated into different blocks. Each block was so long that one couldn't see the end of it. One block for each nationality—Arabs, Pakistanis, Sudanese, Ethiopians, Bangladeshis, Filipinos, Moroccans, Sri Lankans and then, finally, Indians. Most of the Indians were surely Malayalis. Naturally we were taken to the Indian block. It was full of bald-heads and stubble-heads. The length of the stubble varied according to the time of arrival. It was a good sight. It felt like I was a part of a Thursday fair of bald-heads. Our block was very crowded and there was too much commotion. Here, the notions of discipline, quiet and fear that the word jail evokes didn't exist at all.

Hameed and I felt very lost in that crowd, like two foreigners landing in a city for the first time. It took some time for the truth to sink in—that I was finally in prison. For no apparent reason, I wept for a while. It was after days of deliberation, reflection and calculation that I had resolved to come to prison. Despite its harshness, I had concluded that prison was the best option to survive my circumstances.

Yes, I landed myself in prison because of my desire to live.

Can you imagine how much suffering I must have endured to voluntarily choose imprisonment!

Two

We got used to the ways of the prison within a short time. The commotion we had witnessed when we first came in was post-lunch activity. Prison workers were busy collecting plates. Lunch here was served immediately after *dhuhur* prayer. We missed lunch that day. However, compared to the suffering I had endured, regretting a missed meal seems ludicrous.

The prisoners chitchatted languorously into siesta. Lethargic after the meal, many slept. The block didn't have cots, mats or mattresses. One just found a spot on the bare floor. For someone used to luxuries, the heat must have been unbearable; the purring of the three or four ACs set pretty high on the walls provided little relief.

There must have been about two hundred and fifty people in our block. The prisoners, lying down in whatever space they could manage, resembled dead bodies laid out after a natural disaster. Those who weren't asleep, sat in circles and talked. After noting the two new arrivals, someone from a Malayali-looking cluster looked up to say, 'Don't worry, most of us here are Malayalis. Join any group you like,' and returned to the discussion.

Hameed and I found a corner and sat there on our own, not joining any group. Exhausted from the long journey and lack of sleep, we started to doze off almost immediately. But, before long, the azan for the *asar* prayer sounded. Here and there, people woke up and sluggishly headed towards a space set aside for prayer. We also joined them. Along with the others, we turned our faces towards Kaaba to pray to Allah, the merciful.

Bismillah al Rahman al Rahim . . .

While in prayer I could feel my past miseries flowing out in a torrent. I wept tears of joy as I recalled the affection of merciful Allah who had protected me all through my ordeal and helped me journey through the long sandy expanse of misery!

As I got up from that prayer offering all my sorrows and happiness to Allah, the bell rang. The sleepers woke up and took their position in the queue that was taking shape at another corner of the block. Although we didn't know what it was for, we followed the crowd. As the queue moved forward, a big tea vessel came into sight. We could pick up a cup, fill it with tea, get two or three biscuits from the next table, and sit anywhere to have it at peace. When the tea was over, the cup had to be washed clean and returned to the table. It did not seem like being in a prison at all. It was more like a disaster-relief camp. Inside the block, one could walk and talk freely. I had desperately craved for this in the past three or four years—the chance to talk to someone. Just to exercise my newfound freedom, I kept chatting with Hameed. I didn't give him any opportunity to speak. I talked greedily. My tongue didn't remain still even for a second. Hameed, who knew me well by now, lent me his ear most patiently. I must have repeated the same stories to Hameed several times over. But I wasn't satiated.

By the evening, someone from the nearby Indian block came to visit me. I don't recall his name now. As soon as he saw me, he shook my hands and smiled. 'Allah is compassionate,' he said, as if to himself. He enquired if I was the one who had made it to Kunjikka's shop. I nodded yes.

'I know. After hearing about you, I went there to see you once. But you were asleep and I didn't wake you up.' Again he shook my hands and said, 'Allah is compassionate. I came here only two days ago—a scuffle with the sponsor. It's all right. Kunjikka will bail me out.' He kept talking. Every so often, he would clutch my hand and praise Allah a hundred times. I started to weep. And, I don't know why, that stranger also wept with me. Then, praising Allah, he returned to his block.

After that, many others from that block came to visit me. No one asked me anything. They had heard my story from that stranger. They only wanted to see me, and they looked at me in amazement. Some shook my hands and consoled me. Those were in my block also heard my story from those who had visited me.

Breaking away from their groups, most of the Malayalis in the block gathered around me. Some gazed at me as at an alien, some with wonder, some with awe, some with pity and a few with suspicion. Anyhow, I learned that within a few hours I was the topic of conversation among all the Malayalis in the prison. In the days that followed, many more came to see me and made me speak at length. I didn't offend any of them—I fed my insatiable appetite for talking. I mentally revisited every moment of my story a thousand times and my mind and feet were ablaze as if I were walking on burning sands.

That evening, as we sat for dinner after *maghreb*, all the Malayalis in the block were with me. I didn't have anything to give them in return for their love, except some tears.

Three

In the jail, meals were served after different prayers. After the early morning *subahi* prayer, a glass of milk for everyone. At nine o'clock tea was ready and could be had any time until breakfast which was khubus and daal curry. Around noon, after the dhuhur prayer, lunch was served. It was always some kind of Arab biryani called *majbus* or *kabsa*. It was brought in large plates, one for at least ten people. We would sit around the plates in Arab style and eat. The meat in the biryani was different every day: chicken, mutton, camel. When it was mutton, I wouldn't eat that meal.

'What is past is past. Forget it and try to eat something.' 'There is no place to improve health like the prison. We must return at least as we landed here. Don't make your wife lament on seeing you when you return. Only we need to suffer what we have endured.' Hameed tried to console me with such words. Despite all the kind words, I couldn't be consoled. Even the word mutton made my eyes moist.

In the beginning, I would realize that it was mutton in the biryani only after touching the food on the plate. I would then just shake it off my hand, get up and go away. Later, I began enquiring in advance. On the mutton days, I wouldn't even sit for the meal; I would restrict myself to the tea and biscuits served after asar. It was the same at night. When khubus and meat were served in the meal between the maghreb and *isha* prayers, I would back off if there was mutton on the plate. If I was very hungry, I would dip the khubus in water and eat. I had no difficulty in eating khubus without a curry. That had been my diet for many years!

Sumesi jail did not have any of the oft-heard characteristics of a prison. We led a very free life within the block. Maybe we had such freedom because those sentenced for serious offences were housed in another prison or in a different block. In our block we had lawbreakers who were without visas, those whose visas had expired, or those who did not have pathakas, and Muslims who had been out on the streets during prayer time or prepared food during Ramadan, those who smoked in public places, engaged in black magic and had minor scuffles with Arabs and the like. Those with petty or minor sentences and those condemned to be exiled.

I don't recall such carefree days ever in my life. We had food at fixed times, prayed, slept enough and more, reflected pointlessly, talked as much as we liked, and dreamt about our future. The world didn't know us. We didn't know the world either. That was prison.

Hameed only complained about the lack of a facility to bathe. I laughed when I heard him mumble to himself, after a week in prison, about the clammy air and increasing body odour. Then, I calculated with my fingers. Three years, four months, nine days. I laughed aloud again when I thought about it. Maybe even Hameed wouldn't have understood the meaning of my laughter.

Everyone who ended up in the jail had a story like mine to tell—of pain, sorrow, suffering, tears, innocence, helplessness. Perhaps you have heard similar stories elsewhere. I don't want to belittle the pain of others. For each, the path he travelled was harsh. The losses were such that no one could ever compensate for them. I even felt that the sorrows in my life were small compared to the sufferings of some others. In fact, some of these agonizing accounts helped me to come out of my own grief and made it possible for me to continue living to tell you this story. Otherwise, under the weight of my sorrow, I would have committed suicide. A way to come out of our sorrow is to listen to the stories of those who endure situations worse than ours.

*

Every week there was an identification parade in the prison. It was the day for the Arabs to identify the absconding workers—a tear-filled day in prison. On that day, after breakfast, all of us were made to stand in a line outside the block. Arabs would walk in front of us looking at each face carefully, like eyewitnesses trying to identify the accused. There would be a few unfortunate ones among us each week. The first reaction of the Arab who recognized his worker was to land a slap that could pop an eardrum. Some even unbuckled their belts to whip the prisoners till their anger subsided. The policemen would keep an eye on the scene from a distance, and might not even pay attention. Knowing this, some prisoners who spotted their sponsors from a distance, lost all courage and cried loudly. It was only then that one realized how a man becomes a coward when he feels completely helpless. For him, the jail must have provided relief from the suffering he had been enduring. For many, it was inconceivable to return to the Arabs who had been torturing them. They must have endured so many beatings before they reached the jail.

But the Arabs didn't have any compassion or consideration. They would immediately take the prisoners away shouting accusations: he ran away after stealing my money; he tried to rape my daughter; he tried to kill me. The prisoner's face would reflect the abjection of a goat being led to slaughter. His loud cries protesting his innocence would soar above the jail walls; it would be a cry in the wilderness. The Arabs could execute the law as they pleased.

The Arab enjoyed more freedom inside a prison in his country than we did outside in a foreign land. On these parade days, any Arab could freely move around the Sumesi prison if he carried a paper showing that he had registered a complaint in a police station. If he managed to find his absconding slave, he could drag him out and present him before the jail warden and submit his petition to him. The nature of the case would change. The man who was in prison for a petty case would be turned into a criminal offender. It was then either the shariah or the law of the court. The Arab could even demand that he be allowed to take away the prisoner, or that the prisoner be expelled from the country. Here, expulsion was salvation. If the prisoner was ordered to return to the Arab, his fate was sealed.

Remembering my own experience, I shuddered to think what the Arab would do to the absconder. One could only pray to Allah to strengthen those unfortunate ones so that they are able to survive even that ordeal.

On parade day, the block would be eerily quiet. We would grieve for the loss of friends who had been with us in the block till then, sharing food, talking, smiling and playing, dreaming of homeland. Our ears would be ringing with their long howls from the main hall and beyond. No one would be in the mood to eat, drink, talk or sleep. By the time that pain faded, it was parade day again. That day would be the lot of other innocents. Prison wasn't entirely pleasant a memory after all!

Hundreds of Arabs would cross our parade line in those two hours till lunch. During the first few parade days Hameed and I were terrified. Two hours of agonizing fear, not knowing when misfortune would come in search of us. Even the shadow of a likeness resulted in incredible tension. The fear would only go when we became sure that it wasn't anyone familiar.

Although we had to wade through the tears of many unlucky ones, we felt great relief when that two-hour ordeal ended. Forgive me for my selfishness, but I felt glad that no one had come looking for me. Maybe it was the routine nature of its occurrence that the tension slowly began to fade on parade days. Maybe it was the confidence that the reasonable time frame for anyone to come looking for me was over.

Anyone absconding from his sponsor was likely to end up in the police net within a fortnight, or, at the most, within a month; otherwise, he was thought to have found a safe haven. It was considered impossible for any Arab to find him then. There were many who stayed on without any documents. As they were aware of this, the Arabs would give up their search within a month or two. A complaint would remain registered with the police. If he was found after all that, then the Arab was lucky—that's all.

As we crossed that period, Hameed and I were relieved. Nobody was ever going to come searching for us. And being in the line became an amusement and a diversion. Casually talking and cracking jokes, we idled those two hours away. This was our way of dealing with our situation—we had arrived at a compromise with the fear that had once overwhelmed us. This was true for all those who had spent four or five months in the jail.

Our block was like a railway station where people arrived and departed. There were no permanent residents. All the prisoners didn't come at the same time; they came separately, from different police stations from various corners of the country, on different days, at different times. We sometimes didn't even discern the slow inward flow. But some departures were like the emptying of a platform when a train arrived.

The day after the inspection by the Arabs was the day of the embassy visit. Embassy officials of different countries came to the prison with release papers for the prisoners of their respective countries. If the previous day was one of tears, the next was one of joy. On that day too, all the prisoners would be taken out in a line. Embassy officials would read out the names of those whose papers—exit passes—had been processed, and they would step forward. It was a rather impatient wait. It amused me to compare it to the anxiety of beauties waiting for the announcement of the Miss Universe contest results. A joy similar to that which lights up the face of the winner when her name is announced must have erupted in the heart of each one whose name was called out. That roll call marked the final release from a long agony. But nobody expressed it openly. There were many more for whom the waiting—wracked with anxiety and hope—continued. There was despair when one recognized that one's name wasn't among those that were called out. Some, who had been waiting for months, would just burst into tears.

The five-minute period after this announcement, when the officials went into the prison office to take care of the paperwork, was for us the time of goodbyes. It was the time to recall with tenderness our life together, the many days spent with each other sharing each other's griefs. Still, it was with great jubilation that those left behind bid farewell to those who departed. It wasn't possible to say goodbye to too many. Because, by then, the policeman's whistle, like that of the moving train, would go off. All those called would run towards the exit. Who would like a policeman's belt smack his back as he leaves prison?

Four

I felt an intense fear creep into my heart as I spent many days like that in the prison. Those who came before me and after me had left for the homeland. My papers alone were yet to be processed. I knew those who were released had passports and other documents. It was not reasonable to expect the processing of my permit to be as fast as theirs. Still, there was only so much time one needed to get the papers in order. It was already four or five months since I entered the prison. My only solace was that Hameed was there with me to share my misfortune. His papers hadn't been processed either.

Every week, we would have great expectations when the embassy officials arrived and we would suffer greater disillusionment when they left. I had surrendered myself to the police believing Kunjikka's assurances that he would take care of all the rest. It will be taken care of. I must trust Kunjikka. My God

. . . who else will I trust in this world if I don't trust Kunjikka? In Your mercy, forgive me for doubting him even for this half a second of despair, and for forgetting all the favours he did for me in Your name.

These are embassy matters. Everything will happen only in its turn. I have waited and endured for so long. What is another day or two? The time Allah, the merciful, has set for me has not yet come. That was the satisfactory explanation for the delay.

It was that day of the week when the Arabs came to the prison. By then, Hameed and I had become veteran inmates. Since the new arrivals worried more about the Arabs coming in, Hameed and I pacified them as we walked past them to stand at the end of the line. By now, we had become familiars to the policemen. I thought they felt some sympathy for me after hearing my story. Because of that we didn't have to be as disciplined as the new ones. It had become our habit to talk, laugh indiscriminately and make fun of others, while we stood there.

I was saying something to Hameed when his facial expression suddenly changed. Surprised, I looked at him questioningly. For some time, he stood like that. 'Oh Najeeb . . .' he cried in a faint voice. I don't know how many emotions were solidified in that cry—sorrow, fear, hurt, pain. It was only then I learned that so many emotions could coalesce into a single cry. One of life's raw moments that no artist in the world can capture.

There was no need for Hameed to say anything else. I looked towards the spot on which his eyes remained frozen. An Arab was walking towards us. Even before he reached us, Hameed began to howl. And because of that, the Arab did not have to wander searching for his prey. The one he came looking for was there, crying loudly in front of his eyes.

As soon as he saw Hameed, the Arab jumped at him like a cheetah and rained blows on him. He beat him with his hand, his belt and the *iqal* which secures the *gutra*, till his anger subsided. Like the others in the block, I could only watch and cry.

'I wanted to go home. I could not bear to be there any longer. Let me go . . . leave me . . . leave me . . .' Although Hameed screamed, the Arab dragged him to the room of the warden.

That was the last time I saw Hameed. Though I wondered what happened to him, I could not trace him. How many lives like that end halfway, incomplete! Helpless creatures who fade away, unable to recount their stories to anyone.

The familiarity of a few days, much friendship—that was Hameed for me. He had worked in a farm from dawn till night, undergoing torture for low wages. He ran away when it became unbearable. When he reached the prison, Hameed was four times happier than I was. He strongly believed that once he had reached the safety of the government, he would not be caught by the Arab again. But how suddenly does the world turn upside down! That day, the whole block was silent. He was dear to everyone. He mingled with everyone like they were his own. Cracked great jokes. He was like an elder brother to many. Finally we had to see him being dragged away howling. I could not recall anyone in the recent past who had protested so loudly when taken back by an Arab.

It was what happened the next day that hurt even more. Hameed's was the first name to be called out that day by the embassy officials. Oh my Lord, you had not allowed for this name to be called last week. If it had been called out, his life would have been so different and joyful. No. I am not going to contest your judgement. I firmly trust in your exactness.

If you would speak to him and convince him that the time of suffering you have ordained for him has not ended.

When Hameed left, I felt very lonely in the prison. I could not be very friendly with the newcomers. I confined myself to a corner, hardly talking to anyone. I began to eat infrequently. In fact, most days I didn't eat. The loss of Hameed was the loss of my happiness. I would wait anxiously and briefly feel revived when the embassy people dropped in once a week. When we approached them to ask about our papers, they would narrate stories of many complicated papers being processed. They left giving us hope, every time, that everything would be ready by the next week. Thus, I waxed into hope and waned into despair in a regular cycle.

Many such days passed in prison and yet another parade day arrived. I was standing in the queue without any particular fear or anxiety. Many Arabs kept walking past us. Then, suddenly, a face appeared at the farthest end of the line. As that face came into view, thunder rumbled through me. I called Allah just like Hameed had done a few days ago!

It was my own *arbab*, who I firmly believed would never come in search of me. Arbab! My arbab whom

I met for the first time at the Riyadh airport some four years ago. I was dizzy with fear. I thought I would fall down as I grabbed the hand of the person standing next to me.

Desert

::::::::::::

Five

The dust of discord in the Gulf region, generated by the first Iraq war, had somewhat subsided. After a brief lull, there was again an upsurge in job opportunities in the oil kingdoms. When a friend from Karuvatta casually mentioned there was a visa for sale, I felt a yearning I had never experienced before. How long have I been here, diving for a living? How about going abroad for once? Not for long. I am not that greedy. Only long enough to settle a few debts. Add a room to the house. Just the usual cravings of most Malayalis. Not just that. There was a rumour that sand mining from the river was going to be regulated. If that too is gone, what work can I get? Can one go hungry? I have, in the past. But things are different now. Now, at Ummah's insistence, I am married. My wife is four months pregnant. Expenditure will now mount up like a mound of sand. Moreover, I have recently developed a recurring cough and cold—

perhaps from staying in the water for long stretches of time. Can one refrain from diving into the water fearing pneumonia? This must be an opportunity from the Lord Himself. I should not waste it.

'Tell me if there is anyone who wants to go. It is through my brother-in-law. He's here on vacation. If money is sent, the visa will arrive within two months,' my friend said. The passport which I had applied for yielding to Sainu's coercion came to my mind.

'Yes. There is someone. Don't give it to anyone else,' I said excitedly.

'Then come to the house tomorrow. Together we can go and see my brother-in-law. You can discuss the rest with him.'

When the friend left, there was a tension in me. Should I, or shouldn't I?

For a long time, I wrestled with it in my mind. I told Sainu only when I could not resolve it. She was ecstatic—a likely reaction from any woman. 'It is a God-sent opportunity, *ikka*, do not waste it. How long have I been telling my brothers about this, and nothing has happened.'

Both her brothers were in the Gulf.

'But, Sainu, a lot has to be spent. Do we have . . .?'

'If one is resolute, everything will happen, ikka. Do all the people who go have enough money to start with? You go ahead and boldly meet the man from Karuvatta.'

She is like that. Her tongue would not utter even a single word of despair. She's very smart in creating the facade of plenty even in severe poverty. Women should be like that; she was my secret pride.

The very next day, I went and met my friend's brother-in-law. He asked for thirty thousand, twenty to be given to him within a fortnight before he left for the Gulf. He had to give that to the Arab to process the visa. After getting the visa, the remaining ten had to be given to the agent in Bombay for the ticket and other expenses. That was not an amount that I could put together without difficulty. Still, daringly, I agreed. Yes.

The struggles I had to undergo the next one week! Every Gulf worker who had no relative in the Gulf to support him will have a similar story. I finally fixed up the total by mortgaging the house and the little gold Sainu had as jewellery, and by collecting small amounts from other sand miners and by borrowing from everyone I knew. Yes, 'fix up' best describes it. Suffice to say I gave my friend's brother-in-law the money the night before he left. (I could have asked Sainu's brothers in Abu Dhabi, but she refused to let me. She resented them for not helping me till then.)

Two months passed, months of waiting and dreaming. Then there was another round of borrowing. I had to arrange the remaining ten for the agent. Even that was fixed up. Meanwhile, I dreamt a host of dreams. Perhaps the same stock dreams that the 1.4 million Malayalis in the Gulf had when they were in Kerala—gold watch, fridge, TV, car, AC, tape recorder, VCP, a heavy gold chain. I shared them with Sainu as we slept together at night. 'I don't need anything, ikka. Do return when you have enough to secure the life of our child (son or daughter?). We don't need to accumulate wealth like my brothers. No mansion either. A life together. That's all.'

Maybe the wife of every man who is about to leave for the Gulf tells him the same thing. Even so, they end up spending twenty or thirty years of their lives there. And for what reason?

Finally the telegram from the agent in Bombay arrived: 'Visa ready. Come with the balance amount.' The joy that I experienced then! It was greater than the joy of the tens of thousands of Malayalis who had reached the Gulf before me, I am sure. Nobody would have embraced his wife like I held Sainu that night. But one sorrow remained. My son? Daughter? I would not be there for the birth. I wouldn't be able to massage Sainu during her big pain. As if to make up for that, I kissed Sainu's growing belly. My Nabeel, my Safia—names I had chosen to call my child; my *kunji*, my *chakki*—pet names I had for them. Oh my son . . . my daughter . . . Your *uppah* will not be near to see you come into this earth with wide eyes. But, whenever I return, I will bring enough presents for you, okay?

When I recall those moments, I feel nauseated as though from the stench of a fourth-rate film scene. Some situations in our lives are even more absurd than a film scene. Isn't that so?

It was when I went to convey the news of the arrival of the visa to my Karuvatta friend that I learned that another boy from Dhanuvachapuram had also got a visa along with me, through the same brother-in-law, to work in the same company. Neither of us knew much about the outside world. It was decided that we would go together.

I met my fellow traveller as we boarded the *Jayanti Janata* from Kayamkulam to Bombay. A tall and thin lad who had not yet sprouted a moustache.

'Son, Hakeem has never been outside. You are going with him. Please look after him,' Hakeem's mother wept at the window of the train. I did not heed the tears of Sainu and Ummah. I was reluctant to sob in public.

I was more tense than excited. The journey was fraught with all the worries that creep up when one thinks about the difficulties along the way: worry about the money in the bag, worry about the city that one is going to, worry about the stories of fraudulent agencies, worry if my friend Sasi would be at the railway station to receive us. For three days, I feasted on my worries, not wasting any. I even devoured Hakeem's worries. He was only a boy. He was all laughter and play during the journey.

Once I reached Bombay, all the worries vanished. For anything that I needed, Sasi was there, as though he was my own. One has to acknowledge the camaraderie of Bombay Malayalis—Sasi even gave up two days of work for me. We stayed with Sasi and eight others in a room. They had no difficulty in accommodating us. The occupants would not have complained even if there had been two more people. Such magnanimity was only possible among Bombay Malayalis.

It was only after they showed me my visa that I gave the money to the agency. We had been in Bombay for two weeks. A long fortnight. A fortnight when time refused to move. A fortnight when I was made to feel that every second was a century and every day, an age.

Once Sasi and his friends were off to work, Hakeem and I would wander about. We just walked, not knowing the locations or the destinations, and without a language in which we could speak with the citizens of Bombay. That was some bravado. We walked through the shanties of Dharavi. Passing narrow and long *galli*s, one day we reached Andheri railway station. Two weeks of watching the commotion of commuters, eating *paav bhaji*, drinking sherbet, drinking beer—for Hakeem, soft drinks—with Sasi, visiting dance bars and returning late at night.

Finally that day arrived. I did not have much luggage. Some lemon pickle and some *upperi* that my pregnant Sainu had fried with love. Some *chammanthipodi* which Ummah had pounded, disregarding her exhaustion. Pickle of freshwater fish. Two or three sets of clothes ('Why, ikka, you are going to a land where everything is available in plenty'), a bath towel, two bars of soap, a small tube of toothpaste, a toothbrush, my passport, the ticket and some Indian currency. That was all. But Hakeem had a bagful. I often thought that the bag contained enough for a family to eat for a century. Sasi and I often poked fun at him about it, but we teased him merely to see his discomfort.

Sasi and another man from the room came with us to the airport. Like all Gulf Malayalis who leave the homeland, we also promised our friends we would arrange visas for them as soon as we landed there and met our Arab. They laughed as if they had heard it many times. Still, a sprig of hope probably sprouted in their hearts. Isn't it on some such hope that the Bombay Malayali pushes his miserable life along?

As a reward for looking after us for a week, I removed my watch—Sainu's brother had given it to me when he returned from the Gulf for the first time—and gave it to Sasi. Then, from a phone booth at the airport, I tried to call home. There was a phone in a Moplah house in the neighbourhood. When the connection finally went through, I told them to give my message to my family.

Everything went off well at that airport. It was only at immigration that some questions were asked. As I did not speak Hindi and the officer did not speak

Malayalam and as a hundred-rupee note was handed over inside the passport, that hurdle was dealt with quickly. It was an Air India flight. Bombay to Riyadh. A four and a half hour journey. So, at 4.30 p.m. local time on 4 April 1992, I landed in Riyadh.

City of my dreams, I have arrived. Kindly receive me. *Ahlan wa sahlan!*

Six

Hakeem and I alighted from the plane into a wonderland larger than what we had dreamt of. At that time, the Arab world was not shown on TV or cinema as much as it is today. I could only imagine that world from the words of those who had been there. Because of that, every new spectacle proclaiming the fullness of their affluence amazed me.

For me, Bombay was worry, Riyadh, wonder.

I could not remain starry eyed in that wonderland for long. We waited outside the airport after finishing the immigration formalities and, as no one came to collect us, we became anxious. All those who had come along with us in the flight had left in the vehicles of their friends, sponsors and companies. There was no one to pick us up.

The agency in Bombay had told us that the sponsor would be there at the airport. The plane had landed an hour late. Had he come searching for us and returned without finding us? Or was he wandering around the airport looking for us? How would he recognize us out of these hundreds of thousands of people? How different I look from my photo in the passport! We could not hope to be recognized with its help. Or had he forgotten that we were coming? Had the agency forgotten to intimate him? A heap of questions accumulated in front of me. As the time of waiting increased, the heap swelled in volume.

Hundreds of Arabs walked back and forth. Men and women. I distracted myself by picturing ourselves in Antarctica instead and imagining those who crossed us as black and white penguins. I would pleadingly look at the faces (into the eyes of the female penguins whose faces were not visible) of each penguin. I am the Najeeb you are looking for. This small boy with me is the Hakeem you are searching for. I communicated to everyone with my eyes and with my suppliant posture. But no one heeded my appeal. Everyone walked away and faded into their busy lives.

Our wait continued. Meanwhile, many planes landed and people of many nations speaking many languages kept pouring in. They too dispersed and disappeared in many vehicles. As the azan for the maghreb sounded, we learned that it was already evening. When we could not find anyone even after the prayer, we walked to a Malayali-looking airport official and told him about our plight. He asked me the name of the company I had come to work for. I had no answer. He asked for the sponsor's number. I had forgotten to get that from the agent. He asked for the phone number of any local person I knew. I didn't know anyone. I had the address of the company of the Karuvatta brother-in-law and I showed him that. It was a place far away from Riyadh. He would not be able to help. 'Anyway, wait. Surely your *arbab* will not fail to turn up,' he said and walked back to his work. So it was from that stranger that I heard for the first time that Arabic word 'arbab'!

Arbab! Arbab! I repeated it in my mind. So amusing. A harmonious sound. Who is that arbab? What is this arbab? Whatever it is, the arbab has to come, only then can we go. Arbab, come fast, how long we have been waiting. Come fast, save us from this fear. Arbab! Arbab!

Another hour and a half must have passed. As I had given my only watch to Sasi in Bombay, I did not know the exact time. I didn't feel like wandering through the airport looking for a clock to find out the time of the day. What was the use of that? What if the arbab came and left in the meantime?

Outside the airport, the city had begun to travel into night. Our panic began to consume us. Then, an old vehicle—not a car, jeep or lorry (it was after a long time that I learned that it was called a pick-up)—rumbled in and stopped at the main entrance of the airport, even though it was a no-parking area, and an Arab jumped out of it. As soon as I saw him, I don't know why, my mind whispered that he was the arbab I had been waiting for. Impatiently, he walked to and fro in the airport for a while. Although our eyes were following him incessantly, he did not see us. He paced restlessly. I didn't have the courage to go up to him and enquire whether he was my arbab. That thought might never have occurred to Hakeem. Anyway, in which language would I ask him? After going around the airport for four or five times, he found us. We moved towards him.

'Abdullah?' He pointed his finger at me. I had never heard such a crude voice before. I shook my head. 'Abdullah?' He pointed his finger at Hakeem who also shook his head indicating a no. Then he asked something in Arabic. There was anger in his tone. Luckily, I didn't understand anything, Hakeem, even less.

Leaving us there, he went around the airport again. From time to time he would grab the passport of anyone who stood alone and look at it. Finally, he came back to us. Then he snatched my passport and looked into it. Similarly, he snatched Hakeem's passport. Then, without saying anything, he walked forward. Carrying our bags, we followed him.

I had associated Arabs with the fragrance of *athar* and other perfumes. Hundreds of Arabs had walked past us wafting enticing fragrances. I had joked to Hakeem some time earlier that a new perfume could be made by distilling the urine of the Arabs who use perfume every day. But my arbab had a severe stench, some unfamiliar stink. Likewise, while the other Arabs wore well-ironed, pristine white clothes, my arbab's dress was appallingly dirty and smelly.

Whatever it is, an arbab had come for me. I was relieved by that thought. I too have become a Gulf NRI. I too have an arbab of my own. The one who walks in front of me is the custodian of all my dreams, the visible god who would fulfil all my ambitions. My arbab! Arbab—at that moment I could not have liked any other word more!

Seven

The arbab's vehicle was the oldest that I had ever seen. Its doors and bonnet were loose, rusty and badly in need of a coat of paint. As their locks did not work, the doors were fastened with rope. Springs peeped out from the seat cushions.

As we neared the vehicle, the arbab grabbed my bag and threw it into the open back of the vehicle. Arbab! The fish pickle prepared by my mother. The lemon pickle prepared by Sainu . . . My heart burned. Before his bag was snatched, Hakeem placed it at the back of the vehicle. He had many more bottled items—pickles, coconut oil, etc.

The arbab opened the driver's seat and jumped inside. In fact, the cabin could hold only one more besides the driver. Me and Hakeem together? Well, we would have to adjust. As I went to open the other door, the arbab yelled out something. Startled, I took a step back. The arbab pointed towards the back. I remained where I was, continuing to hold the door handle, as I did not understand anything. Again, he pointed and shouted, '*Ya, yella!*' Then he opened the door angrily, came out, grabbed me by my hands and pulled me to the rear and pushed me up the back of the vehicle. Seeing this, Hakeem jumped in. The arbab hurried back to his seat and started the car.

In the back of the vehicle there were two or three large aluminium vessels, some grass and many sacks. We somehow managed to fit in, holding on to the side rails. Despite its antique appearance, the vehicle was pretty fast, we felt. Its growl and grumble were too much. However, we realized its true speed only when we left the airport and touched the main road. Hundreds of vehicles kept overtaking it heartlessly. The only thing it overtook was the dark smoke its exhaust pipe breathed out.

My first journey through the Gulf streets. Although it hurt that it was in an open vehicle, it was only because it was open that I could unreservedly enjoy the resplendence of the tall illuminated buildings on either side of the road. Could I have ever seen the Gulf in its fullness like this if I had been sitting with the arbab in the front seat? As it was already dark, nobody travelling in the other vehicles could see us.

I have no idea how long that open-air journey lasted. Hakeem had no idea either. The radiance of the metropolis grew fainter. I could make out the long road parting from the city. The number of vehicles overtaking us decreased. Soon, the intermittent neon glare from the street lamps became the only light. After some more time, I noticed we had deviated from the highway. Distant street lamps were the only source of light. Hakeem had dozed off somewhere along the journey. He must be weary, let him sleep, I thought. I realized that our journey had moved to some sand road by now. Light transformed into an envelope of dust. Then, darkness. Raising dust, the vehicle sped between sand dunes.

The only thing that had gone into my stomach till then was the little water that I had had on the plane. I had been feeling too nervous when Sasi compelled us to have breakfast before we left. I could not eat the plane food either as I was not sure about how to eat it. I was actually starving. With the blistering hunger that one experiences after a mining session in the river. When I mentioned it to Hakeem at the airport, he said that he felt as though he might die of hunger. I wanted to howl, arbab, please stop, get us some food, some water . . . But nothing came out of my throat. It would not come out. I was afraid. Afraid, that I would anger the arbab. Not only that. It was pitch dark and there was no sign of any place where food might be available. An hour must have passed since we had started driving on the sand road. My back began to ache from the jerks and jolts. The rising dust made it impossible to breathe. What kind of a journey is this, my Lord, I cried involuntarily.

From that moment, like the *maniyan* fly, an unknown fear began to envelop my mind. An irrational doubt began to grip me, a feeling that this journey was not leading me to the Gulf life that I had been dreaming about and craving for. The Gulf I had learned about from so many people was not like this. A whiff of danger. Nothing clear. I would have been at ease had I shared my anxiety with Hakeem. But he was fast asleep. Let him sleep. If he listened to my worries, he might start crying.

There was no way to know the time. I cursed the moment I gave Sasi my watch. Let us reach when we reach. What was the use of knowing the time? I was travelling in the vehicle of my own arbab. In his hands my life was safe and secure. Why should I worry about the time? I lay down and slowly sunk my head into a bundle of grass. Up in the sky, the stars hid their lustre. They were asleep. I lay there, staring idly into the emptiness of the sky. The unending jolts and the growl of the vehicle entwined composing a lullaby for my fatigued ears. I fell asleep.

Eight

It was only when the arbab shook me that I awoke—to eye-piercing darkness. I had no idea where we were. It took my eyes some more time to adjust to the darkness. Hakeem was still in deep slumber. Again the arbab angrily struck the rails to make a loud noise. As Hakeem scrambled awake, the arbab signalled to him to come out. When I collected the bag and started to follow, the arbab made it clear that it was not me but Hakeem he had called. Still half asleep, Hakeem couldn't understand much. The arbab growled like an angry wildcat.

We are two poor things, arbab, who do not know anything at all. Why are you angry with us like this? Do you know, arbab, we're hungry? In fact, more thirsty than hungry. I cannot remember a single day of starvation like this. What a great reception this is, coupled with your needless fury. No, why should we accuse the arbab? Wouldn't he also be hungry and thirsty? He must have set out many hours ago to pick us up. At least we travelled by plane. He had to drive this old vehicle to the airport and back. At least we managed to sleep a little in the plane and in the vehicle. The arbab had had no sleep. Only after taking us to our place can he eat a little, drink a little water and stretch his back. Be angry, arbab. Be furious, even. We are guilty of sleeping without even realizing that the vehicle had stopped.

I sensed that we had reached a plain, with not a building or tree anywhere in sight. Far away, like a map, some mountains or hills, silhouetted against the dark sky, could be seen. A cry sprung in my heart: My Lord, where have I ended up?

Hakeem jumped out with his bag. The arbab led the way in the darkness. He seemed to know the place. Hesitantly, Hakeem followed him. But didn't Hakeem and I come to work in the same company? Weren't we supposed to live together and work together? Why did the arbab bring him here in this darkness? Why am I made to remain seated in the vehicle? Where is he taking Hakeem? My Lord, his ummah had left him in my care. Rogue arbab, where are you taking Hakeem? I jumped out of the vehicle resolutely. I took my bag and ran after the arbab and Hakeem.

The arbab turned back. Even in the darkness I could see his eyes redden with rage. I asked him something in Malayalam. His furious gestures failed to drive me back to the vehicle. Then he unbuckled his belt and swung it in the air once. Its blood-curling whoosh was frightening. Reluctantly, I returned to the vehicle.

Open plains have some light even in the dark of the night, some sort of a radiance from the remains of light that shatter against the sky from the ends of the earth or other places. As my eyes became accustomed to that light, I could see the arbab stop in front of the gate of an iron-mesh enclosure. I saw him pull out a key from his pocket and take Hakeem inside. Although I was intensely curious to see what was going on inside, it was too dark for that.

The only thing I could discern in the air was a foul smell, maybe the arbab's stench. I had the common sense to understand that we had been driving through the desert. Was it the smell of the desert? Do deserts have such a smell? The deep sea, they say, does. The air was filled with that smell. I had been conscious of it since the vehicle stopped. Initially I thought it was because of the dust raised by the vehicle. But now it was clear that it was coming from the iron enclosure into which the arbab led Hakeem. Like the mixed smell of bone powder and dung. Have we reached some bone-powdering factory? If so, where are the buildings? The machines? The heaps of bone? The exhaust pipes? Where? Who knows?

I waited for the arbab to return. Fear had really taken possession of me now, a feeling that I had entered into a dangerous situation. It was as though Hakeem had been imprisoned by the arbab and that it was my turn next. He might have plans to lock me up in some dungeon. I would run before that, escape from this danger. But where to? All around there was only a vast expanse of nothing. Since I was unfamiliar with the terrain, if I tried to run, not knowing the direction, or the way out, I would die wandering in this desert. I was hungry and thirsty. How much distance could I cover? Yearning to run, yet refusing to move, I remained seated at the back of the vehicle.

After some time, the arbab came out alone. He locked the gate from the outside. I jumped out of the vehicle, ran towards him and enquired about Hakeem. The arbab frowned at me and walked to the vehicle. He told me something as he walked. It was in Arabic and I couldn't understand anything. The arbab got into the vehicle. Hurriedly, I returned to my position in the back.

The vehicle stopped again after travelling hardly a kilometre. This too was an open area. Carrying my bags, I followed the arbab. At some distance, a tent became visible. I realized that this was my arbab's destination. I didn't see any light except the natural light of the wilderness. As we reached the tent, another arbab, also in Arab attire, came out. A short arbab, like a caricature from old Arabic stories. His clothes and stench his were worse than my arbab's.

They talked for a while. Then, handing me over to the new arbab, my own arbab went back to the vehicle. I relaxed a bit as I figured out that he had probably entrusted Hakeem with some arbab like this. He was a naive boy. I was afraid that he had been locked up in some dark room.

Outside the tent, one could see a long iron fence. Like the compound into which Hakeem was taken, this too was a source of a foul smell. There were some unidentifiable movements. Pointing towards them, my new arbab went back into the tent.

I felt deeply sad. My arbab, how can you so cruelly walk away after leaving me here in this darkness in front of a tent, without saying a word? Don't you know that I am here in the Gulf for the first time?

'Have you eaten? Are you thirsty? Are you hungry?'
Shouldn't you have asked me at least that much?
Shouldn't you have shown me where I should stay
and introduced me to my co-workers? Is this the
legendary Arab hospitality that I have heard about?
What kind of arbab are you, my arbab? Don't deceive
me. In you rests my future. In you rest my dreams. In
you rest my hopes.

I don't know for how long I stood there like that.
Did I expect that my arbab who had left would return
with some food for me? I might have. But as soon as
I realized the futility of waiting, I walked towards the
place the arbab had pointed at.

My accommodation must be there somewhere.
But there was no sign of a tent, let alone a building.
Inside me, something burned to cinder. If my arbab
lies down in a tent in the middle of the desert, where
am I going to stay?

Worried, I paced along the iron fence. I could see
some shadows move, moan and jump inside the fence.
Then, as if to acknowledge my presence, I heard a light
whimper. It was the bleat of a lamb! I peered inside
the fence. Goats! Hundreds of goats! Rows of goats,
undulating like a sea. It struck me like a thunderbolt.
I had a rough idea of my job now.

After that distressing moment of panic, I sauntered along the fence. I only took three or four steps ahead before a cot, along the fence, became visible. A man sat on it, with bowed head. Seeing that figure, I was petrified.

Nine

Shaking slightly, I walked towards that scary figure. He had matted hair like that of a savage who had been living in a forest for years. His beard touched his belly. He had on the dirtiest of Arab clothes. Also that horrible stink that can drive anyone away! Although he saw me coming, the figure didn't move. For a moment, I was confused. Was it a statue or a human being? Then quite unexpectedly, he chuckled. It became a long rattling laughter. I couldn't fathom its meaning or relevance. After laughing for some time, he said something in Hindi. Because my schooling ended after fifth class, and because I never had any occasion to pick up Hindi, I didn't understand what he said. Arabic might have been more intelligible to me than that Hindi.

There was pity in those words, and also sadness, resentment, scorn. Today I understand: he was lamenting my fate and wailing. Compassion doesn't require any language.

Then the figure fell down like a log and went to sleep. After some time, I could hear snoring.

By then, I was somewhat aware of the situation I had ended up in, and about the nature of my job. I shuddered for a second thinking about becoming another scary figure. I should escape before that happens. Where to? Anywhere. How? However. Now, this very moment. The arbab must be asleep in his tent. The scary figure is a dead wood here. Nobody will see me. If I run . . . how long will I run? Which way . . .? In which direction? To which place? I don't know anything. When I thought about the hours we had travelled from the city, a fear was kindled in me about the place I had reached. I was chained to that place by that very thought.

The night had advanced. The night breeze of the desert had the chill of the month of Makaram back home. The gruelling fatigue of travel hit me, to say nothing of hunger and thirst. Sleeping at nine after dinner had been my habit back home. In that open expanse, I became numb without a place to sleep or sit. Then, as my legs began to ache, I placed my bag near the scary figure's cot and sat on it. Gone were the thoughts of the pickles packed by my ummah and my Sainu.

As I sat there, feeling utterly consumed by hunger, thirst and exhaustion, I could make out a large tank near the fence and, near its base, two or three valves. Grasping one in the dark, I turned its head. Ah! Cold water began to gush out. Greedily I gulped the water, till I was satiated, till I was full, till I had had enough for the next day and the day after, as if I was afraid I wouldn't get any more. Oh my Lord, how can I explain the relief I felt? For a while I sat there before the tank, exhausted. Then I got up and went back to the scary figure's cot. When weariness overtook me, I laid down on the sand, using my bag for a pillow. My back ached. I smiled at the emptiness. What dreams I had had! An AC car, an AC room, a soft mattress with a TV in front of it! I laughed. What else could I do in my present condition? No one else could have realized how far my dreams were from the reality of my situation. My first night in the Gulf was such a fiasco.

*

It was the commotion of the bleating of hundreds of goats that woke me up in the morning. The day was already very bright though the sun was yet to rise. I got up slowly. My body ached terribly from sleeping on the sand. I had a vague recollection of fishing out a sheet from my bag and covering myself with it. It was there in the sand, crumpled. The fearsome figure on the cot was not to be seen. I thought maybe it had been a nightmare.

I sat on the cot and looked around. There were many more goats than I had expected. The fence encircled a large area that was divided into many segments, and in each segment there were hundreds of goats. Beyond the fence, the desert stretched out as far as the eye could see, touching the horizon. There was not even the shadow of a tree to block that sight. On one side was a fairly large hill. Everywhere else there were only sand dunes rising to the height of two to three men. They made the otherwise flat surface uneven.

After some time, as if to prove I had not dreamt him up, the scary figure came out from among the goats. It was only then that I could clearly and closely see how terrifying he was. Dust had transmuted into scales on his body and dirt matted his beard and hair. His dirty fingernails had grown crooked and looked hideous. It must have been five years at least since his last bath, and a century since his clothes had been washed. A century!

He came to me with an aluminium bowl full of milk. After he poured out some milk from it he gave it to me and told me something in Hindi. It was hot like it had been on a stove. I wondered if a goat's udder was so warm. Thinking that he was asking me to drink the hot milk, I gulped it down. I felt the pinch of hunger from the previous day and emptied it completely. The scary figure pulled my ears and mumbled something. Tried to ask me something. Tried to sound angry. When his words shattered against the barrier of language, helplessly he gave me another bowl of milk and gesturing with his hands he told me to give it to the arbab.

I went into the tent of the arbab with that vessel of milk. Lying on a cot, he was not much different from the scary figure: dirty, wearing stinking clothes. No sign of the benefit of taking baths. He woke up and yawned. Then, taking the bowl from me, he finished it in one go. The vessel must have contained at least five litres of milk!

Handing back the bowl, the arbab asked me something. As usual, I didn't understand a thing. He tried his best to communicate in Arabic. Not even a word of it entered my head. Furiously, he stamped his feet on the ground. All of a sudden, all the grief I had been restraining gushed forth as tears. I howled loudly in front of the arbab. Maybe it was the overflow of the sorrow, anger and hunger that filled me. I was wailing 'I have to go', 'I cannot be here', 'I did not come for this work'. Although I knew that the arbab didn't understand a thing, I felt that it was my duty to say what I had to say. I hoped that he would take pity on me, seeing me cry. Instead, he irately pushed me out of the tent. Weeping, I went and sat on the scary figure's cot. The scary figure was busy with some work. I did not care. My eyes and mind were filled with tears.

Whenever he came out and went back among the herds of goats, the scary figure kept telling me something, while continuing to work. I could make out that he was trying to explain the situation to me. Maybe he was consoling me, sympathizing with me. But I was astounded by the absolute indifference that seemed to have permeated his voice and his facial expressions.

The day became brighter. Even the morning sun was quite harsh. The scary figure opened the gate of the fence, let the goats loose and followed them. I was left alone.

Then, my own arbab, who had dropped me here the previous night, came in a pick-up. It was similar to the previous day's vehicle, but better looking, a big vehicle that would fit a joint family. It was only then I noticed that the previous day's vehicle was parked at some distance. Last night, the arbab must have returned in his own vehicle.

I was somewhat relieved when I saw my own arbab. I ran towards him. There were no traces of the previous day's anger on his face. But, without acknowledging me, he took out something from the boot and walked towards the tent. Like a dog wagging its tail, I followed him. The two arbabs embraced and greeted each other for almost five minutes after which they began to talk. While doing so, they glanced at me from time to time. I guessed that their conversation was about me. Finally, the arbab who had spent the night in the tent gathered some things, put them in the boot of the car and left, after a final salaam.

Ten

I was still waiting outside the tent, crying. My own arbab came towards me, patted my back and said something to console me. Although it did not console me, it mitigated my wailing. He went back into the tent, opened a packet and gave me something that looked like a chapatti. 'Khubus,' I heard him saying clearly. This, then, is khubus. I had heard this word in the riverside bragging of many Gulf-returnees. Khubus.

The arbab signalled to me that I should eat. I had not even brushed my teeth in the morning, nor followed any of my morning rituals. I hadn't taken a bath. Had it been at home, I wouldn't even drink coffee without first ducking into the river—even when it rained. But that day, for the first time, I violated all my hygiene rules. I had drunk milk without brushing my teeth. Hunger for one and a half days forced me to ignore my habits. I sat outside the tent and greedily ate the new dish called khubus, even though I had nothing to dip it in or to smear it with. I didn't feel the need for it either. It had the warmth and sweetness of freshly baked bread. Every time I took a bite, my mind kept repeating 'Khubus! Khubus!' After devouring four, the name engraved itself in my mind and in my stomach—khubus.

When I had finished, the arbab brought me a glass of water. I guzzled it down. Then he offered me another khubus. I declined. My stomach was full and I was fully satisfied. I was touched by the arbab's affection.

By then, the scary figure had returned with the goats. He drove them inside the fence. Then he came and sat in front of the tent. The arbab gave him five or six pieces of khubus. Dipping them in water, he gulped them down, drank a jug of water, and went away without saying a word. I had observed the scary figure's face as he sat eating. I saw a life hardened by sorrow and pain. He continued with his work, ceaselessly, without a moment's rest.

The arbab went inside and brought me a *thobe*—the dress of the typical Saudi Arab man, a long, white, shirt-like garment, loose fitting, long sleeved and extending to the ankle, usually made out of cotton—and a pair of boots. I unfolded the thobe and almost

vomited from its musty reek. It was unspeakably
dirty. The arbab touched my pants and shirt and said,
'Sheelaadi . . . sheelaadi.' When he repeated it many
times, I understood that he was asking me to remove
my clothes. I undressed and reluctantly wore that
stinking garment. I removed the brand new leather
shoes I had brought from home and stepped into the
stinking boots. It was my initiation to the stench, the
first step to becoming another scary figure. Although
I could foresee my dark future, I obeyed the directions
of the arbab, so grateful was I for the khubus he had
given me a while ago.

Pointing at the scary figure, the arbab said
something in Arabic. I could only catch the word
masara. Guessing that masara meant water, I dutifully
took a pail and followed the scary figure. I filled
the bucket with water from the tank, went inside,
walked through the goats, and poured it out into
a large container there. It was a cement tub, about
three metres long, a metre wide and a quarter metre
in height.

There were about twenty to twenty-five sections
within the fenced area housing about fifty to a hundred
goats each. In every section there were tubs for water,

raw wheat, grass and hay. The goats could eat and drink whenever they wanted.

When the tub in the first section was filled, the scary figure opened the gate of the second section and released the goats. Leaping and bounding, they surged out. As he followed them, the scary figure pointed at a tub and said something in Hindi or in Arabic. The only word I could make out was *mayin*.

Mayin? I wondered what it was. Water or bucket? If it was water, then what was the masara that the arbab had mentioned? Who knew? Whatever it was, my job was to fill those tubs with water. So I did just that. Before he came back with the goats, I had filled the tub in that section.

Similarly, I filled water in the third and fourth sections. It was not easy. My back began to ache from carrying the bucket filled with water. Besides, as the noon sun blazed, the heat became oppressive and I grew thirsty.

When he was about to take the goats out from the next section, the arbab came out of the tent and told the scary figure something in Arabic. He concurred, nodding his head. Then the arbab came over and handed me a long stick. I received it with both my hands. It felt as though I was going through my initiation ceremony as a shepherd.

Together we herded the goats towards the wilderness. After we had walked for some distance, the arbab clapped his hands to call me. I walked back to the tent where the arbab placed something in my hand. I looked at it—as far as I could make out, it was a pair of binoculars. I had no clue as to why he had given it to me. Thinking that it was meant to find runaway goats, I prepared to go back with it to the desert. '*Shuf . . . shuf . . .*' the arbab prompted me to look through it. I was curious. I was holding a pair of binoculars for the first time in my life. I looked through its twin lenses. Oh, how clear everything looks! I marvelled. Objects that were kilometres away appeared so near, so clear. Even the marks on the goats were plainly visible. I looked all around. I was happy. 'Shuf?' the arbab asked. I nodded in agreement. He grabbed it from me and took it inside the tent.

Then he lifted up the pillow and drew out a double-barrelled gun. He walked out and aimed at the sky. A bird was flying high up. He aimed at it and fired a shot. Bingo. The bullet hit the bird and it fell. The arbab smirked at me. I was petrified.

'Shuf,' the arbab repeated.

I nodded.

'*Yella, roh* . . .' the arbab pushed me after the goats.

That moment, I realized that my life had become inescapably bound to those goats.

Eleven

Casting off the previous night's thoughts of escape, I walked into the desert. I remember: it was only sheer emptiness that filled me then.

The scary figure was far ahead of me by that time. I looked at the desert stretching out before me. This place was quite different from deserts I had heard about or seen in pictures. The word evokes in us waves of sand. But it was nothing like that. It was all hard soil and boulders. I had seen a similar landscape when I had been to the eastern parts of Kerala. There was only one difference. And a big one. Unlike in our place, where vines spread through the rocks and sand, there was not a speck of green here. It was a sterile wasteland. I could not help but wonder why these goats were taken out. Though the goats were instinctively sniffing for grass on the ground, they got nothing.

After a while, I caught up with the scary figure. Leaving the goats to roam, the scary figure sat on a boulder. I sat on another—I didn't have anything to do, and I didn't know what to do. I wanted to ask him about so many things. But how? The only language that I had was that of signs, and he was not even looking at me. What was he gazing at? Neither at the heavens nor at the earth, merely into emptiness, I thought. After some time, he got up and herded the goats together. It was a somewhat difficult task. There were about a hundred goats. When one ran this way, the other headed in the opposite direction. By the time they were somehow beaten back to the fold, yet another would have run away. After gathering every goat with some effort, the scary figure began to walk back towards the fence. As I didn't know anything, I merely watched.

Together, we reached the enclosure. When he told me something, I guessed he meant 'You proceed to the masara with the goats, I'll follow.' Ah, then masara means the enclosure for goats. So, mayin must be water. At least let me learn the words like that.

I brought the goats to the enclosure. He came with the grass. Together, he and I brought water and hay to the masara. Did I say masara? Look how quickly I switch to Arabic.

We went to the next masara and took its goats to the desert. It was only after we had taken the goats of two or three masaras that I became conscious of the purpose of these excursions—these goats were not taken out to be grazed, but merely to give them some exercise. A limb-stretching morning exercise to cure the lethargy of their daily existence.

The sun began to blaze furiously. All the goats had been brought back from the daily jaunt. Every one of them had been supplied water and feed. Then, an awful thing happened. The call of nature became severe. I hadn't performed the early morning bodily needs. The last time I had managed it was before boarding the plane in Bombay. It hadn't been necessary the previous day as I hadn't had anything to eat. But the four or five khubus I had consumed in the morning began to have an effect. But where could I do it? I didn't need the screen of four walls. At home, the riverside or a bush cover was good enough. One could also wash in the river. But, here, there was not even that minimum privacy. It was wide open all around. It is true that everyone did it and everyone knew that everyone did it; still, as humans we expect some privacy for certain actions of ours, don't we? I was apprehensive about sharing this with you. Then I decided I must, merely to explain how apparently trifling issues agitate and distress us. If such private dilemmas are not laid out in the open what is the use of telling a story?

I tried to calm myself. But this was not something that I could suppress. With every second, the discomfort increased in my stomach. Slowly, I walked to the other side of the masara. There was now at least a screen of goats between me and the arbab, and between me and the scary figure. That was more than enough. Closing my eyes, I did it.

Relief. The utmost relief that one could get in the world.

I rose up after throwing some sand and stones on it, like a cat. I needed to clean up. That was not difficult. There was plenty of water in the tank. I could carry some in a bucket and clean myself behind the grass or hay bales. I collected water in a bucket and walked behind the bales.

Before the first drop of water fell on my backside, I felt a lash on my back. I cringed at the impact of that sudden smack. I turned around in shock. It was the arbab, his eyes burning with rage. I didn't understand. What was my mistake? Any slip-up in my work? Did I commit some blunder?

The arbab snatched the bucket of water from me and then he scolded me loudly. Lashed at me with the belt. When I tried to defend myself, he hit me more ferociously. I fell down. The arbab took the bucket and went inside the tent.

This was what I gathered from the arbab's angry words in between lashings. 'This water is not for washing your backside. It is meant for my goats. You don't know how precious water is. Never touch water for such unnecessary matters. If you do, I'll kill you!' Thus I learnt my first lesson. It was wrong to wash one's backside after taking a dump.

I got up, feeling very uneasy. I had never faced such a predicament in my life. It was almost as if I lived in a river. Without water, nothing happened in my life. Cleanliness had been my ideology. I would get annoyed when Sainu didn't bathe twice a day. And I was always in water! But the breaking of all my habits began that day, didn't it? The harshest for me was this ban on sanitation.

I came back and sat on the sand, below the cot. The scary figure was sitting on his bed, eating khubus. He handed two or three to me. I couldn't imagine eating anything without cleaning myself. I refused to touch the food. Then I saw a sight at a distance. A herd of camels, about fifty, marching in a line. It was a grand sight. The first time I saw a camel. The largest in front, and the smaller ones forming the tail. There was no one to lead them or herd them. They chose their own path.

As they came near us, I looked at them in amazement. It seemed that their heavy eyebrows signified all the severity of the desert. Nostrils opening and closing like the gills of fish. Broad open mouth, strong neck, coarse hair like in a horse's mane, ears erect and horn-like. I was most attracted to and most frightened by their detached look. I looked into the eyes of one of the camels for a brief second. I retracted my gaze as if I were looking at the sun. It felt as though the depth and the breadth, and the severity and the wildness of life in the desert were crystallized in those eyes. It must be the impossibility of its situation that lies congealed behind the camel's impassive countenance. I would like to describe the camel as the personification of detachment. Those camels went past me and walked inside the fence on their own. It was their own masara.

Twelve

I was deputed to give water and fodder to the camels. I went up to their masara, but I was afraid. Do camels hurt humans? If they do, how do they attack? Kick? Bite? Trample? I had no idea. But I had to enter their masara and give them water and fodder. There was no way I could avoid entering the masara because there was a being more ferocious than a camel could ever be—a dreadful arbab, following me with sharp eyes. I stepped into the masara daringly. Expecting a bite or a kick, I walked in between their legs and somehow gave them water and fodder. Later, I had many more opportunities to learn how the right combination of circumstances can forcibly dissolve any man's fears.

That day the camels didn't hurt me. I had to fill water in four containers, fodder in four, wheat in two, hay in three. By the time my work got over, I was exhausted. With my eyes, actions and supplication, I implored the scary figure to help me. Whenever he stood up to help, the arbab came out and prevented him. Only then did I realize that it was the punishment for taking water to clean my backside.

I went and sat near the cot of the scary figure. When my breathlessness and fatigue subsided, I began to feel hungry. The khubus the scary figure had given me was still there under the cot. I did not worry about the fact that I hadn't been able to clean myself. Couldn't bother about cleanliness any more. Sitting there, I had four large khubus and gulped down two mugs of water.

When I finished, the arbab beckoned me to the tent and advised me and scolded me. While listening to him, I acted as if I understood everything. Even though I didn't understand anything, I could comprehend the magnitude of my crime.

After that, for a brief while, it was rest-time. I searched all around for a little shade, but it was nowhere to be found. All that was left was the glare of the blazing sun and the scorching heat. The little shade there was was in the arbab's tent. He guarded it like it was a sultan's palace, not letting anyone in. I didn't have the nerve to creep in there.

The scary figure slept soundly on his cot, unmindful, a cloth on his face to block the sun. The sunlight and the heat did not seem to affect his grimy body. Folding a towel on my head, I sat near the cot. After braving the heat of the sun for some time, the little rectangle of shade under the cot caught my eye. It felt like the greatest discovery in the world.

Indeed, if the worth of a discovery is measured by its necessity and the demands of one's situation, to me, my discovery was greater than any other. How long had the scary figure been lying in the sun? Why didn't he find the possibility of shade, like I did? Elated, I sneaked under the cot and stretched out. Although the sand was hot, my short nap was more pleasing than the sleep I had experienced before.

I must have dozed off when I was called. Again, like I had earlier in the day, I took the goats out, batch by batch. I noticed for the first time the different types of goats and the different types of masaras designated for them. In one, only milk goats; in another, the male and adult females; there were different masaras for goats of different sizes and lambs of different ages; in yet another, sheep; and in the last one, camels.

The gate to the camel enclosure opened as we were going out with the goats. They went on their way, on their own. When we returned with the goats of the last masara, the camels returned. The chores were repeated—water, hay, fodder, wheat . . .

The scary figure came with a large pail and I followed him as he went inside the masara of the milk goats. He milked them one after another at great speed. In one go, he filled that pail. Together, we carried it out.

The arbab drank some milk from it, and the scary figure had two cups. Although they told me to drink as much as I wanted, I couldn't because of its disgusting odour. The remaining milk was taken to the masara of the young lambs. They gathered around the bucket, as if to drink *kaadi*—a type of cattle drink prepared back home from the water used to wash rice—and glugged from it. Again, I noticed—I had started noticing new things with my eyes and mind—that the little lambs were not kept with their mothers. Mother and child were kept separately. No lamb was allowed to drink straight from its mother's udder. All were given milk in the same bucket. In that case, which mother's milk did a child drink . . .? Isn't it through taste and smell that a child recognizes its mother? It should be like that, whether it be a goat, dog, cow or human being. Is this communal drinking meant to sever the bond a goat and its mother enjoy? Who knows? That is the way of the Arabs, or at least the way of the arbab. I was fated to obey him. Why should I think and worry about anything beyond that?

Shadows lengthened, the sun disappeared beneath the desert folds. Dusk bloomed, night set in. By then, the night-arbab arrived with the night meal. He offloaded some provisions and water from the vehicle. The day-arbab loaded the vehicle with some things and left.

The night-arbab had brought khubus. No curry for it, though. Just khubus. I understood what my menu for the days to come would be.

Early morning drink: fresh, breast-warm raw milk (only if one felt like it)
Breakfast: khubus, plain water
Lunch: khubus, plain water
Evening drink: fresh, breast-warm raw milk (only if one felt like it)
Dinner: khubus, plain water.

And plain lukewarm water from the iron tank to drink in between meals (only when very necessary).

After finishing the night chores, the scary figure lay down on the cot. I spread a sheet on the sand. The arbab was inside the tent. I wanted to ask him many things, but as soon as his back touched the cot, the scary figure started snoring.

I was alone. My bag was my pillow. It had the scent of pickle. Suddenly, I recalled the people at home, Ummah, Sainu, our son (daughter) who grew inside her. They must be troubled not having heard of my safe arrival. I felt miserable. My heart felt like it was about to burst. How will I convey to them that I had reached? That I am fine?

I remembered Hakeem. What work would he be doing there? From far, it appeared that he too had landed in a masara. His situation can't be different. Sad. How many dreams would he have had as he boarded the plane? How can he suffer this at so young an age? He was not very poor. His father was in Dubai. This visa came when they were trying to take him there. 'Yes, go abroad, without wasting yourself at home. Learn the language and life there. Within two years you can be taken to Dubai,' his uppah had told him.

Poor boy, how would he endure this arduous life? In my case, I am used to a hard life, mining sand. It's fine with me. He was only used to fun and frolic back home. What will become of him? These are the designs of Allah. One must endure these things. What

is the way out? The days to come will only be harder.
My Allah, most merciful, grant Hakeem and me the
strength to endure these sufferings.

The night dawned into my second day in the desert.
I slept late that day too, maybe because I was not used
to the sleeping posture I had to adopt.

Thirteen

I was exhausted even before the day began. As I got up in the morning, my hands, legs and body ached. My body hurt more than it did after a whole day's sand mining in the river. More than the pain, it was the irritation of not being able to bathe myself clean after work that bothered me. I would never come out of the river without bathing though I had worked in water the whole day. It was the uneasiness of sleeping in the same dress one wore in the sun, sweating and moving among stinking goats, and being strewn with their urine and dung. My dress stuck to my armpits and in between the legs; to say nothing about my sweat-soaked shoes.

I had hardly woken up when the scary figure handed me an aluminium vessel and gestured that I had to milk the goats. Milk the goats? Me? I could feel a blankness envelop me then. As if I had fallen into a crater of ignorance.

I had never seen a goat so close in my whole life. Okay. You might wonder—haven't seen a goat closely! Where are you from? Yes, you and I have seen goats. Goats have been living in close proximity of humans since the dawn of settled life—from 7000 or 6000 BC. A poor creature domesticated by our neighbours Mariyumma, Janakiamma, Velayudhan Kutty and so on. It is a lovely animal. Anyone will feel like cuddling little lambs. Goats give us milk, little lambs, dung. We can drink the milk, sell the lambs at the Thursday fair, use dung as manure for banana trees. Goats eat leftover food and grass. They drink kaadi. They fall sick if they eat cassava leaves and are happiest eating jackfruit leaves. Beyond that I did not know anything about goats. Perhaps you don't either. Where is their native place? Who are their ancestors? Obviously, I did not know important things like the different kinds of goats, and the qualities of each kind. I was even ignorant about basic details like the number of its teats, number of hooves, duration of pregnancy, period of milk production, how much milk they produce each time, how to milk a goat, how many times to milk it and how to pull its udders for milk. Did they kick with their hind legs like cows or with their front legs like horses? How does one evade its kick? I didn't know anything.

I had never asked anyone about goats. And no one had ever told me anything. Had I known that this would be my assigned job here, I could have observed and learned all about them. Janakiamma who lived only a few paces away had two or three goats. I had seen them too—eating grass by the wayside and in the fields, their little ones leaping and bounding. Maybe they were milk goats. Had I known about my present job in advance, I could have practised milking them. But I had barely noticed them. A lot many creatures live all around us. The situation could hardly have been different had I been called to rear cows or to look after dogs. It is only when we have a need that we think about them and regret that we hadn't noticed, learned or understood them when we had the chance. It was only after falling headlong into this situation that I realized the need to keep our eyes open to our environment.

What else could I do? I had to learn on my own. I entered the masara with the pail and approached a goat. Back home, I had seen the teats of the goats being washed before they were milked. In the desert there was no water even for people to bathe and clean themselves! There was no question of washing the teats. Slowly, I crouched behind a goat, took the vessel close to its udder and pulled at it. Not only did no milk come out of it, the goat squirmed and leapt away into the flock, kicking down the vessel along with me. Seeing it sprinting crazily, the other goats also ran helter-skelter. One of them ran over me trampling my back. I writhed in pain. Somehow, I got up, crouched behind another goat, one that had stopped running. When I touched its teats, it too was startled and leapt away. I tried to milk yet another, and it ran away too. My Lord, I thought, how can one milk a goat that runs? I was baffled.

Feeling determined, I approached another goat. That ran off too. This continued. After half an hour, when the arbab and the scary figure came into the masara to see how much milk I had got, there was not even a drop in that vessel. What's more, I was frog-leaping after the goats.

Seeing my plight, the arbab scolded me and went back to his tent. The scary figure came in and took the vessel from me. Then, he demonstrated how to approach a goat to milk it.

Never approach the goat that had to be milked from behind. Approach it from the front. Do not start milking it straight away. Caress it like a child by tenderly touching its cheeks, ears and back. Stroke its sides, pat its back and then slowly sit by its side. Caress its underside twice or thrice. Then slowly touch its teats. The goat will twitch. Even goats feel ticklish. Like a virgin. Then, ease its discomfort by slowly caressing its teats. At home, its baby would perform this task. And one can only milk after the intimate mother–child contact mitigates the ticklishness and the fondness for the child makes the milk ooze from its udders. There were no lambs here to put the goat at ease and to make milk seep out. We had to do that work too. After ensuring that it has got over its ticklishness, pull the udder from top to bottom using the thumb and the index finger. The pressure shouldn't hurt, but must be firm enough to draw milk. This control is something one masters gradually. It is the mark of a milkman's worth.

Do not try to hold the vessel in one hand and milk with the other. When you milk with one hand, slowly caress the teats with the other. Any jumpy goat will remain still. It will not kick, leap or knock the vessel over.

How the scary figure controlled the goat—I was spellbound by his performance. Those nervy goats, what happened to their annoyance? After milking some goats, he handed me the vessel. Slowly, I mimicked his actions. Of course, it had all the drawbacks of imitation. It was only after some time that I realized that activities such as milking come naturally to an animal lover and animals instinctively distinguish them from their mimics. Also important is the daily contact with the goats. They say that a goat can understand if a new pair of hands touches its teats.

Still, I managed to control a goat and placed my hands on its teats. I cannot explain the satisfaction I felt when the first drop of milk fell into the pail. As if I had completed my training for a big job. I had mastery over one of the many goats that must come under my control. The others will eventually follow.

When I somehow managed to fill half a pail and come out of the masara that morning, I was drenched in sweat, as if I had done some hard labour.

Fourteen

Another day, not very different from the previous, came to an end. Meanwhile, the scary figure had trained me in the many ways of herding goats. He demonstrated how to lead the goats—not from the front, but from the sides; and how to beat into control those that try to break away. He taught me how much wheat, hay and fodder should be supplied in each masara.

That day seemed hotter than the previous one. My throat was parched after every ten paces, and it burned as the lukewarm water from the iron tank travelled down it. Also, because I was not used to the water, my stomach became upset. I don't know how many times my stomach ran that day. Overcoming the previous day's shame, I sat down openly to do it, wherever I felt the need. To avoid being beaten by the arbab for trying to clean myself with water, I began cleaning my behind with stones. I concluded that it was customary for each region to use what was most available there.

The English have plenty of paper, so they use it for cleaning; for us it is water, and we clean with it; here, stones were aplenty.

After midday it became humid. I felt like I was being steamed. Fatigue sunk in, and my running stomach made it worse. I complained to the scary figure and to the arbab, nevertheless, my workload was unaffected. The arbab cared only about my work, not about my discomforts.

I was clammy by the evening, as though I had been soaked in rice juice. My skin felt irritated and inflamed as I hadn't washed for many days. Hiding from the arbab, I washed my hands and face in the water for the goats. My armpits and pubic area, untouched by water, felt filthy.

That night I went to bed uneasy. Of course, when I say bed, I only mean figuratively. My bed was the loose sand. The scary figure had appropriated the only cot there. My bag was under it. I would pull out my sheet and spread it on the sand. It was already dirty, but without it, the small pebbles in the sand would hurt. I had an unpleasant night but given the circumstances, only a fool would expect any comfort.

My discomfort kept me awake even though I was very tired. My thoughts were not of my home country, home, Sainu, Ummah, my unborn son/daughter, my sorrows and anxieties or my fate, as one would imagine. All such thoughts had become alien to me as they were to the dead who had reached the other world. So soon—you might wonder. My answer is yes. No use being bound by such thoughts. They only delay the process of realization that we've lost out to circumstances and there is no going back. I realized this within a day. Anxiety and worry were futile. That world had become alien to me. Now only my sad new world existed for me. I am condemned to the conditions of this world. I have fallen headlong into the anxieties of it, and it is better to identify with the here and now. That was the only way to somehow survive. Otherwise, my growing anxieties would have killed me or my sorrows drowned me. Maybe this was how everyone who got trapped here survived, no?

Can you imagine what I had been thinking about that night as I lay down? About going to the masara early in the morning and milking the goats; controlling the goats as the scary figure did and coming out with a vessel full of milk; the arbab's face lighting up when he saw me with the milk; and single-handedly herding the goats of a masara and bringing them back. On how to go about realizing those dreams, and the precautions I had to take; about what my drawbacks had been that day, and how I could rectify them.

I neither bothered about yesterdays nor worried about tomorrows. Just focussed on managing the todays. I think all my masara life was just that.

Lying on my sheet, I tried to remember the Arabic words I learned that day and their meanings. It had only been two days. But I felt that I had learned more words than necessary.

arbab	saviour
masara	house of the goats
khubus	the only food that I might get here
mayin	a very rare liquid to be carefully used (Please do not trivialize it as mere 'water'. What the arbab feels about mayin is not comparable to our attitude towards water.)
ganam	goat
haleeb	milk
thibin	grass
barsi	hay
jamal	camel
la	no
ji ham	yes, arbab
yaallah	get lost

It was only after recalling these words that I realized I didn't know many more: wheat, vessel, tank, car, gun, desert, dress, bath, shit, loose motion, beating, anger, scolding, tent; and many verbs like came, went, didn't do, do not know, etc.

If an Arabic expert among you asks whether the pronunciation and meaning of the words that I have tabled here are correct, I can only say I do not know. I've heard them like that, and have learned them like that. I was able to imagine a meaning out of those sounds. So, as far as I was concerned, that was the correct word and the correct pronunciation. After all, what is there in a word—it is understanding that is important. I could understand what the arbab meant by those words; and the arbab could understand me. One does not need to be a linguistic expert in order to communicate.

As I lay there thinking and musing over the past couple of days, time flew. Pain evaporated. Along with fatigue, sleep embraced my body. Deep sleep. Surely, it must have been past midnight by then. I woke up only after daybreak. The sun had opened his eyes in the east much before I opened mine. I woke up and looked at the cot. It was empty. He must have woken up early and got down to work, I thought. I ran to the masara hoping to be there before he finished milking. But the scary figure wasn't there.

The goats had not been given water or fodder. The tanks had not been filled with wheat. Nothing had been done. Their routine disrupted, the goats were restless. I thought the scary figure was engaged in some other masara. I went around all the masaras. He wasn't to be found in any of them. I wondered where he could have gone so early in the morning. I came out of the masara and sat on the cot. My mind was plagued by doubt, and I bent down and looked under the cot. The previous day I had seen a very old and dirty bag, one which I guessed was his. It wasn't there! The sprout of suspicion grew.

Then the arbab came out of the tent and walked towards me. He gave me a vessel and asked me to milk the goats and get him milk. I looked at the arbab apprehensively. Surely the arbab must have understood the meaning of that look—where has the scary figure gone? Then the arbab told me a lot of things. His words were loaded with anger, curses, sympathy, cruelty, disparagement.

This is what I could gather from those words: he, my scary figure, had escaped from this hell!

Fifteen

We had been acquaintances for only two days. I don't even know if he could be called an acquaintance. A few words were all that we had exchanged. Didn't know his name, native place, nothing. Still, it hurt a lot when I realized he had gone. I couldn't fathom the reason for that pain. It might have originated from the anguish of intense loneliness. Suddenly my body was overpowered by weariness. Like the sensation one feels when out of the blue one hears that one's uppah or ummah or child has died. But my arbab, the messenger of the dismal news, had no feelings. 'He's left.' Yes, he has. That was all. Where, how, with whom? 'No,' he said, as if he didn't want to know.

Unexpectedly, I saw a ray of hope. The arbab would react similarly if some day he heard that I had also left. If the scary figure is gone, there is Najeeb, if Najeeb is gone, there will be someone else. That's all.

But I was not as hopeful when I saw his attitude
and activities on the first day. He shot at the sky with
his gun, demonstrated the range of the binoculars,
observed me from the top of his vehicle whenever I
went out, and drove around me when he felt that I
had gone too far. I feared he would never let me escape
from this hell. I had observed that fear and precaution
in each action of the scary figure. I could discern that
fear in each word he uttered to me: Never attempt to
flee. He will kill you if you do—that unkind, brutal,
ruthless arbab. But after saying all those things to me,
he had escaped. Liar! He had been waiting for me to
join, had handed over everything to me and scooted.
He served me all those lies so that I wouldn't try to
escape. Look, how calm the arbab is. Even his usual
annoyance is not to be seen. Only an air of resignation,
what's gone is gone.

When I thought about my situation, I felt happy.
One, the scary figure had somehow escaped from
this suffering. Two, I too can escape like this in the
future. Three, and most important, I am going to
appropriate the cot. I would not have to sleep on the
ground again.

As I got a whiff of freedom, I became very lively.
I ran to the masara with the vessel and milked some

goats. Of course, I was still an amateur, but I did much better than the day before and did not get as many kicks from the goats. I had come a long way from the previous day's not-even-a-drop stage. But it would be some time before I was as good as the scary figure.

I gave some of the milk I got to the arbab, the rest I placed in the masara of the young ones. Then, I began the rest of the back-breaking work. I had to do the work of two people. The camels had to be fed and set free. I supplied enough grass, wheat and fodder to each masara, and filled the containers with water. Meanwhile, a water truck came, and I helped the man fill the tank; a trailer came with fodder, and I helped unload it. Although I worked hard, the jobs at hand were never-ending. Even when it was time to herd the goats (I had started guessing time from the length of the shadow), half the masaras hadn't been supplied with grass.

Although the arbab had been watching me work, he scolded me for not taking the goats out. I retorted that without help I could only do so much. The arbab answered me with his belt. A lash across my back. I squirmed in pain. It felt as though that lash would sting and hurt my back for the next six months. As he walked away, the arbab said something. I understood what he said—it was the work done by one person till I had joined the scary figure. At times a strange language can also communicate very well. I ran away crying and finished the remaining jobs. I didn't get time to have breakfast, nor did the arbab invite me to have some.

I had just finished herding the goats of two masaras when the arbab called me and explained that a vehicle had come to take the goats to the market. 'Catch the big ones and load them into the vehicle.' It was my elder arbab who came in the vehicle. There was no one to help. I entered the goats' enclosure. Standing outside, both the arbabs would select a goat and point at it, '*Aadi*.' I would try to catch it, but like a snakefish in water, it would slither away. I would follow it, catch it (How to catch . . . it didn't even have any rope around its neck?), and take it up to the vehicle. The next problem was to push it inside the vehicle. I was not strong enough to carry it in. The goat wouldn't get in willingly. I don't know how much energy and time I spent on somehow pushing each one into the vehicle. By the time I managed two or three, I was worn out. But the arbabs made me scurry to the masara again and again. They would point to the masara and say, '*Aadi abiyad*.' I wouldn't understand which one. Thinking that it was the goat next to me, I would try to catch it. '*Himar, maafi aswad, abiyad, abiyad,*' the arbabs would holler. Realizing that it was not that one, I would try to catch a bigger one. '*Himar, mukh maafi inti, aadi abiyad,*' the arbab would hit my head. Only after many mistakes did I finally realize that the arbab was asking me to catch the white he-goat.

Dragging it out, I somehow pushed it into the vehicle. Again, back to the masara. The arbab would say '*Aswad*,' I would again commit some blunder before finally getting him the black goat he had pointed at. By the time I finished catching about twenty goats, I fell down, exhausted. I cursed myself and many others. The scary figure got his freedom. My reward: back-breaking labour! A lash that I would never forget! Starvation till lunch!

Sixteen

I was learning to face life alone, to train myself in jobs I had never performed before, to try out a new way of life, to get accustomed to an uncommon situation. It was not as if I had a choice; I was utterly helpless. Had we learned that one could get a little water only if one worked till one's bones broke, we would work till we died, not just till our bones broke.

Since I had helped out the scary figure for a couple of days, I was confident that the routine jobs would not be difficult and that I could master them. Only the milking and herding of goats needed a little training; the rest even a blind man could do, all one needed was a bit of health and strength. At least that was my understanding. But, as the days passed, I had to learn many new things on my own—the ways of goats, how to rear them, the habits of camels. Circumstances can make a man capable of learning to do anything.

One day I was taking the goats out as usual—it must have been one week after my arrival—when I noticed that one of the goats looked sluggish and weary. It was pregnancy fatigue—like Sainu's. When I'd asked the arbab if I should take it out, he had nodded his head in permission. After we were half-way from the masara, the goat moved away from the herd and lay down. Puzzled, I stood near it. After a while, it began to moan and squirm. Only then did I understand that it was going through labour pains. Although I tried to make it go back to the masara, it fell down after three or four steps. Meanwhile, the other goats were already scattered in the desert. As long as they moved in a herd, the goats acted fine. However, if the line got disrupted, if the herd scattered, it was all over. Then their instincts took over. Goats are the only domesticated animals that, despite living with man for about six thousand years, slip back into their wild nature whenever possible. That was why the scary figure had instructed me on my very first day to keep them in line and within the herd.

Before I could do anything, fifty goats had gone in fifty ways. I was in a dilemma: should I leave the one in labour and go after the rest or take care of it leaving the others to wander around? Finally, recalling the shepherd who goes in search of the lost one, leaving the forty-nine, I decided to attend to the goat in labour.

Forget goats, I had never seen any animal giving birth. I didn't know what kind of help an animal in labour needed. I had never had any pets myself, nor had I cared for any of the animals that had lived in my neighbourhood. Therefore, my participation was limited to standing there, watching passively. After a while, I saw a head emerging and, with some horror, I continued to watch. Then involuntarily I ran forward to support the baby as it slowly began to come out, ingesting all the flames of pain. But because of the sliminess of its body, I couldn't hold on to it. It fell off my hand, to the ground.

From somewhere, suddenly some old knowledge flashed inside me: the placenta should be removed! I cleaned its face and body with my hand. Its mother was even more conscious of her responsibility towards the kid than me. Within seconds, she licked the baby clean. Soon after its birth the baby began to try to stand up, and succeeded. It slowly tottered to its mother's udders. I saw that it was a he-goat.

At that instant, my mind shook free of all its shackles and everything I had been trying to forget hit home. My Sainu is pregnant. When I left her, she was near delivery and I've had no news of her since. Maybe this was a good omen Allah wanted to show me. My Sainu, my wife—she has given birth. A baby boy, as I had longed for. In that belief, I named that newborn goat Nabeel. The name I had thought of for my son.

My hand and my dress were all wet with the water that broke and the blood from the placenta. Where could I wash? That the arbab would rebuke me if I returned to the masara without the goats was a certainty. I cleaned my hands on my robe and then I lifted that unsteady and beautiful little kid and kissed it. You are the present Allah gave me. Be well, my darling.

I took Nabeel to his mother's breasts. Out of the blue, a swift blow flung me some distance away. Only when I regained consciousness after a few stunned moments did I realize that it was the arbab who had kicked me. He was looking at me with burning eyes and pointing at something as he hollered. The rest of the goats were scattered all over the desert. I mumbled

a few words like goat, delivery, baby, placenta, etc.
But the arbab was in no mood to listen. Angrily, he
came forward and pulled my Nabeel away from his
mother's teats. Then, brutally disregarding my helpless
pleadings and the mother goat's heartbreaking look,
he went back to the masara carrying Nabeel on his
shoulders.

Leaving the mother goat there, I ran after the other
goats. It was only after a great effort that I could
somehow gather them. As I walked back with them to
the masara, the mother goat followed us helplessly.

More punishment awaited me when I got back.
I was severely beaten and reproached. The arbab
accused me on four counts in that day's charge sheet:
one, I had tried to take some water to clean the
placenta and blood off my hands and dress; two, I was
late to return with the goats; three, I had wasted time
by looking at a goat giving birth—goats know how
to give birth and don't need any human assistance;
and, four, that was the most severe crime, I'd tried to
make the newborn drink its mother's milk.

I knew that the young ones were given milk in a
pail. But I didn't know that even a newborn was not
allowed to have breast milk.

My reward for trying to help a goat deliver her baby was severe words, a kick, enough spit, two or three belt whippings and starvation at noon.

Even then, I didn't feel bad or sorrowful. I was sure that Allah would bestow my real reward back home on Sainu and my son. Or so I told myself. I needed to hold on to something to survive.

Seventeen

I gave more care and affection to Nabeel than to any other goat in the masara. Maybe, he didn't have any need for it and he would have been fine living with the other goats. But I couldn't let him go. He was the one who was born into my hands, the gift that Allah had given me in place of my son. Unseen by the arbab, I would often make him drink from his mother's breasts—a good fortune no other goat in the masara ever enjoyed. What better gift could I give him than making it possible for him to drink from his own mother's breast? While the rest were fed from the common pail of milk, I made him drink separately. I fed him tender leaves of grass, making him walk by my side when the goats were taken out. Like a naughty boy, he would break away and spring ahead, and turn his head to look at me. I would run to catch him and he would shoot into the herd and hide. And when I caught him, I would kiss him. For me, Nabeel was not one of the many goats in the masara. He was my own son.

He was very naughty from the beginning. It was his habit to fight with he-goats bigger than him. Some goats would accommodate his friskiness, but some would strike him with their horns. How many times he came to me bleeding! Unseen by the arbab, I would take water from the tank and clean his wounds and apply on them the medicine the arbab had. Nabeel recognized and returned the special treatment and affection I gave him.

One day, after eating khubus, I was about to take the goats for a walk when the arbab called me. No outing today. Today there is some other work to be done.'

After some time, the arbab came out of the tent with a long sharp knife. Inside me, something burned. My Lord, did he plan to kill some of these goats and eat them later?

You couldn't ask the arbab anything. You could only just listen to whatever he says. You must obey whether you understand his words or not. That is what I had been doing so far. Therefore, I was afraid to ask the arbab anything. I quietly followed him.

The arbab went near the masara where the little he-goats were kept. Looking at one of the he-goats, he directed me to catch it. To kill it, I was sure. Murderer! But I was not brave enough to oppose him. Unwillingly I entered the masara and brought the he-goat he wanted outside. He asked me to turn it to face me, place its body between my thighs and to raise its hind legs. I didn't have a clue as to why I had to do that.

The goat was soon standing on its forelegs, its body between my thighs and its hind legs in my hands. The arbab, who was right in front of me, could see the underside of the goat clearly. The goat was trembling with fright. I was even more scared. I remember that the arbab made sure of the sharpness of the knife. Then there was a wild cry like I've never heard before and I saw blood squirting, as if from a spout. In my hands, the lamb wriggled with all its strength. For a second I feared I would lose my grip. 'Don't let go,' the arbab yelled. Fearing the arbab's wrath, my strength defeated the goat's. In the next second, the arbab took out the spray from his pocket and aimed it at the wound. Even then the goat continued to cry with all its life. But the bleeding, as if by magic, stopped abruptly. After a while, the goat's writhing body relaxed. The arbab indicated that I should return it to the masara. When I released it at the gate of the masara, it bolted into the herd like a wild boar that had had a shot fired at it.

Pity! A he-goat had lost its maleness. A maleness that was to the arbab a small piece of meat and a little blood. I had noticed that not all male goats were allowed to live with their virility. Only a select few were lucky. After a certain age, they were made to live among she-goats. They could mate as they pleased and enjoy all the male pleasures. The rest of the he-goats were castrated and made into eunuchs. They were meant for slaughterhouses. I'd observed that the castrated male goats grew faster, but I had not realized that castration was so brutal.

The arbab pointed at another goat and commanded me to fetch it. I entered the masara and caught it. The arbab knew the age of each one and also when to destroy their maleness—some in the first month, some when they were two months old. By measuring its male endowment, the arbab was able to discern whether a goat would be able to produce active and healthy offspring that grow up to give plenty of milk. That was the basis on which the decision to allow it to retain manhood or to castrate it was made.

I kept on fetching the goats he pointed at. Casually, like paring one's nails, the arbab kept slicing off their manliness. My heart was shaken when he pointed at one of them after finishing with five or six. That hand pointed towards my Nabeel! I was shocked! My Nabeel? You, who I hoped would grow up in joy! My son? No, I cannot abandon you to his knife. I could not. I pushed him among the goats and caught another one as if the arbab had pointed out at that one. But the arbab's eyes were like a vulture's—although he lay idly inside the tent, he knew each of his goats like the lines on his palm. 'Not that, the other one,' the arbab's hand stretched out towards Nabeel. I could not catch him. I could not do him such harm. Again I caught the legs of another one nearby.

'Himar!' the arbab yelled. That was the very end of the arbab's patience. Next would be the heavy kick on my back, I knew. Still, I caught another one the third time. The arbab leapt at me and kicked me on my back. I was thrown aside. Angrily, the arbab caught Nabeel's legs and dragged him out. I rose and touched the arbab's feet. Oh arbab, please let him grow to become a he-goat. I need him. I would not like to send him to the slaughterhouse. Let him live here with me. I begged him in all the languages that I knew.

'Himar!' The arbab struck my head. 'I can recognize the ideal he-goats. Only the kids they breed will be strong. Only they grow fast. What do you know? He has to go to the slaughterhouse soon.' Without any mercy, the arbab dragged Nabeel out and commanded me to raise his hind legs. Then, in the blink of an eye, my Nabeel's manhood also fell on the ground, soaked in blood like that of many other goats.

The cry that came from Nabeel when he was cut! Even now it echoes in my heart. It felt like my heart was being lacerated with a piece of flint. I only remember Nabeel whining and running into the masara. Then, when I woke up, I was lying on top of a bundle of hay. It was already afternoon. The arbab gave me some water to drink and then sent me to do my routine chores. The day Nabeel lost his manliness, I too lost mine. I haven't yet figured out that mystery—of how my virility vanished with that of a goat's!

Eighteen

You would think it is not difficult to take the goats for a walk. That we only needed to gently guide them from time to time. In movies you might have seen them moving in groups, walking close to one another. There would be a leader to lead them. Where the leader went, the rest followed. The goat that is very familiar with us would be made the leader and it would then be that goat's responsibility to lead the rest of the goats and lambs. I named the three head goats in the masara Lalitha, Ragini and Padmini.

But in reality it is nearly impossible to manage goats. They walk and bound off in all directions. If one went left, the other would go right. I had to simultaneously herd some fifty to a hundred goats at one go. These goats have a mind of their own. I think I explained their habits sometime earlier. Although they have, like sheep, been living with humans for about six thousand years, we did not have such a hard time domesticating any other animal, and we haven't still succeeded entirely. Among them, the he-goats were impossible to control. A full-grown one would be almost as big as me. When they are let loose among females to mate, they lose all control. The vigour of the he-goat in heat—running through anything and everything—is certainly a spectacle worth watching.

One day, while taking them for a walk, I hit one of them just once from behind. It turned back, like a cross elephant and snorted with all its might. I saw fumes coming out of its nostrils. The next moment, it charged at me, and without giving me a chance to evade, hit me right on the chest. It felt like as if a one-tonne mallet had hit me. I only remember flying off for some ten metres, like a villain hit by the hero in a Hindi film. I fell unconscious and don't know how long I lay there like that. Then, when I opened my eyes, the arbab was in front of me. All the arbab did was pour some hot water on my face. Then he called me himar and shouted something.

Somehow, I scrambled up and looked around—the goats were scattered in a perimeter of nearly five kilometres. I became conscious of a terrible pain in my left hand. An immense unbearable pain. The hand was swollen. I told the arbab that my hand felt broken. He removed his belt and hit me, and shouted at me to run and fetch all the goats quickly. The arbab warned me that it would be my end if even one of them was lost.

I ran through the desert, literally carrying my throbbing hand. The goats were enjoying their unexpected freedom to the full, revealing all their wild characteristics. It was like a nation in slavery waking to revolt suddenly. Absolute chaos. When I somehow brought a goat to a side, the one already there would have run off. When I ran after the second, the first would have wandered off again. After a few tries I realized that it was impossible to gather all of them at one go. I began to run to the masara with the few I managed to collect, lock them up and rush back to the desert. Then, with the five or ten that I managed to gather, I would return to the masara again. The first goat would be about two kilometres away from the masara, and the rest scattered at about five kilometres from there. I am not sure how many times I had to cover the distance between the masara and the desert. I only remember that I was dead tired. And when I stopped to have some water, the arbab hit me hard, snatched the cup of water from me and flung it away. I rushed back into the desert again, thirsty, panting, my tongue parched.

Looking up at the sky with anguish, I whimpered the name of Allah all through that exercise. I could see goats scattered till the horizon. How was I going to get there? My feet were swollen, pain pierced my hand relentlessly and my thirst was severe. Screaming and shrieking, I ran after the goats. There was not even a hint of a wind, all was still in the sky and there was the blazing sun.

It was afternoon when I brought all the goats back into the masara. Later, I would often wonder how I survived for such a long time in that scorching heat without even a drop of water and with no rest at all. The two factors that helped me through that phase were my desire to live and my infinite faith in Allah. After bringing in the last goat, I fell on the cot, thoroughly exhausted.

The arbab came and sat near me and dripped some water into my mouth. 'Water . . . water . . .' I mumbled over and over again. Even in my half-conscious state I heard the arbab saying you people are profligates, profligates who do not know how to use water carefully. Then I lost consciousness.

It was night by the time I woke up. My hand was even more swollen and the pain was too severe to bear. I was sure it was broken. And my chest hurt from the pounding from the he-goat. My throat felt like it would crack from the thirst. I walked unsteadily to the water tank and drank to my heart's content. Then I went to the arbab's tent. Scolding me for sleeping for so long, he threw two or three khubus at me. I was very hungry. Dipping them in water, I greedily finished the khubus. I couldn't sleep a wink that night because of the pain. I went crying to the arbab's tent several times. I begged him to take me to any hospital. But the arbab didn't pay any attention. As dawn broke, he came to my cot with a vessel and asked me to hurry up and milk the goats. I showed him my hand. I got a smack on my head as a reply.

The pain on my chest hadn't eased and my hand was inflamed by then. I limped to the masara in that state. How could I milk the goats with just one hand? My usual practice with well-behaved goats had been to place the vessel on the floor and milk them with both the hands; the impish ones needed a rub on their back. What could I do with only one hand? If a goat jumped, it would kick the little milk I managed collect. Blindly, praying to Allah, I entered the masara. The first goat I saw was the one I had named Pochakkari Ramani. How I gave it that name is a story I shall tell you later.

I looked into Ramani's eyes and told her, 'Ramani, I cannot move my hand at all. It is the work of one of your partners. But the arbab must drink milk in the morning. It doesn't matter to him if my hand is broken or if the sky has fallen. He must drink milk, and I must get it to him. If you cooperate, I will escape the beatings of the arbab. My fate is in your hands today.'

To tell you the truth, I have often felt that goats can understand things better than some humans. Anyhow, that day, Ramani stood still for me. Somehow, I got enough milk for the arbab and placed it in front of his tent. I cursed him in my mind: Drink pig, drink till you are full!

After gulping down the milk the arbab came to me and asked me to hurry up and milk the goats for the young ones. I simply wasn't capable of that. I openly told the arbab, 'I can't! Can't! Can't!' I think I was screaming by then. The arbab saw this side of me for the first time. He was really shocked. I went and lay face down on the cot, expecting belt lashes on my back. At the most, the arbab would kill me. Let him. This torment would end. What fear remains for one who is willing to accept death? Allah, I had promised to you and to your law that I would never commit suicide.

I hope you will have no objection if I leave myself to be killed by the arbab. I am not fated to see my son. It is okay, I am not sad. Let me die at the hands of the arbab. I cannot take this suffering any more.

But the arbab did not come near me as I had expected. Already the goats had become restless and were jumping around. They were used to a schedule. If their routine was disrupted they got jumpy. Let everything go to hell. What do I care? I lay still.

When the elder arbab arrived, I did not get up. The two arbabs talked to each other. After that the day-arbab came towards me, took my arm and examined it. He massaged it through the swelling. Consumed by pain, I screamed loudly and begged the arbab to take me to a hospital. But he took his vehicle and went somewhere, as if he hadn't heard me at all. I stretched out on the cot. He came back after some time with some herbs in his hand. Mashing them in a vessel, he applied it on the swelling, and then, like in olden times, took some sticks and fixed them tightly around my hand with a cloth bandage. I showed him the puffiness on my chest. There too he applied the herbs. All through the ordeal, I kept begging the arbab to take me to a hospital. All that the arbab said was 'It is okay, you will get well soon.' I did not trust him. I was afraid that my hand would worsen, rot and would have to be amputated.

The arbab brought me two or three khubus. Dipping them in water, I swallowed them. 'It is already pretty late, quickly take the goats for a walk,' the arbab ordered. I couldn't say no. I ran to the masara, holding my broken hand.

By about noon, I could feel the pain slowly ease and fade away. It almost disappeared completely by night. Within just a couple of days, the swelling was gone, both on the chest and the hand. About ten days later, the bandage was removed. All those days, I milked the goats and took them for walks, with only one good hand. To my amazement, during that period, the goats never kicked or charged at me, or even toppled the milk pail.

Maybe goats understood me better than the arbabs ever did. They must have realized that I would never hurt them even if they charged at me. However, I kept a safe distance from the he-goats. I evaded them if they came towards me, or I protected myself with my staff. I never got attacked by a goat after that horrible incident.

Let me tell you something that I have not divulged so far in this story. Would you believe me if I told you that my childhood ambition was to become a goatherd? Maybe, it was a wish born out of seeing the movie *Ramanan*. My ummah loved *Ramanan*. To wander about from one land to another. To saunter with flocks of goats through meadows and hillsides. To pitch one's tent every day in a new place. To sit by the fire guarding goats on winter nights. Shepherding was for me what dreams were made of.

When I finally got the chance to live the life of a shepherd, I realized how painfully distant it was from my dreams. We shouldn't dream about the unfamiliar and about what only looks good from afar. When such dreams become reality, they are often impossible to come to terms with.

Nineteen

I lived on an alien planet inhabited by some goats, my arbab and me. The only interruptions to the monotony of my life were the visits of the water truck twice a week, the hay truck once a week and the wheat trailer once a month. These vehicles were the only means by which I could connect with the outside universe. The drivers were usually Pathans from Pakistan. If I established a connection with those people, I could contact the external world. I could at least inform them that I existed. They could be the means for my eventual escape from here. A faint flicker of hope that I would have such a chance to slip away slumbered somewhere in the corner of my mind. But the arbab used to send me off to the desert early on the days when they came with instructions to return with the goats only after they left. On most days, I didn't even have to help them fill the tank and unload bundles of hay and grass, and sacks of wheat.

Still, my heart would flutter with inexpressible joy whenever those vehicles reached the masara. I'd be elated, as if some loved ones had come to visit us. I would chat with the goats more than usual. But when those vehicles, raising dust, faded away, I felt like the world itself had run away from me. Then a heart-draining fatigue would come over me.

Unexpectedly, one day, a trailer came without any helper to unload. The arbab called me back from the desert. The driver was a Pakistani. I saw a man who wasn't either of my arbabs up close after a very long time. Since I had been denied normal human smells I felt that even his sweat had a scent. Out of the sheer happiness of seeing a man, I even touched him once. I felt a shiver of satisfaction passing through me.

While unloading the material, I explained to him all my sorrows in all the languages that I knew and begged him to somehow save me from the hell I was in. However, I saw only icy coldness in his face. He didn't even acknowledge me. The anguish I felt! When the arbab had called me to the trailer, I had run to him with so much hope, deserting the goats. It was an optimistic dash towards the light of life. But the driver's cold look drained me of all hope. I looked at him pathetically whenever he placed the bundles of hay and grass on my head and tried to attract his attention with some gesture. I begged him to save me. Once I deliberately dropped the hay bundle and bent down and touched his feet. Even then, he wouldn't look at me. I felt sad. My heart broke.

After unloading the goods, the Pakistani drove away without even smiling at me. My optimism dimmed. How much I cursed him! Nobody in the world would have ever cursed a stranger like that or hated one like that. To get rid of some of that anger, I hit my own chest twice as I walked back to the desert to gather the goats.

Today I can understand the vulnerability of the driver who must have known the arbab for years. One cannot say what the arbab would have done if he had tried to talk to me. One time, the arbab jumped out with his gun when the driver of the wheat trailer tried to talk to me. I remember the arbab felling the driver of the water truck with his rifle butt for trying to talk to me. How many goats like me must have got trapped in this masara before? Maybe the miserable outcome of trying to save one of them must have been fresh in the Pakistani's mind. Maybe he, sitting in his vehicle, was crying his heart out for forsaking me so heartlessly. Even if that wasn't the case, I preferred to believe so. I tried to convince my heart so. It was only thus that I managed to swim across many of my sorrows. Merciful Allah, I am fated to walk through these harsh days that you have ordained for me. Forgive me for hating and cursing that innocent man for that.

*

In the beginning, everything in the masara had a nauseating stench. The smell emanating from goats' urine, the stench of the droppings, the reek of grass and hay that got wet with the urine. If I had ever experienced a similar stink before, it was in a circus tent.

Even the goats' milk had that stench. Whenever I dipped khubus into the milk to eat, the smell would drill into my nostrils. How many times I vomited in the first days. But slowly, it retreated from me. Or I forgot about it. Later, although I tried many times, I could never experience it. It became so much a part of me I could not believe that such a stench had ever existed. Not only that, I was able to discern the difference in the many smells that originated from the goats. The he-goats had a special smell and the sheep another. There were hundreds of types of sheep, each with a distinct smell. Pregnant goats had a certain smell; goats about to give birth had another. Based on that smell, I was even able to calculate a goat's date of delivery. The newborns had a particular smell different from that of older lambs. Goats in heat had a different smell. The smell of the camels was distinct from all the rest. There are two types of camels—those with one hump and those with two. Each type smelled different. There was only one animal in that masara without any smell, and that was me.

One day, I developed a craving to write a letter to Sainu. I didn't bother about how it would reach her. I had to write. I had to. During the brief interval after the khubus-and-water lunch, I dragged out my bag from under the cot. The letter pad and pen I had brought from Bombay were inside it. I took them out. The pen began to write faintly only after a lot of scribbling. I was writing a letter for the first time. I had no idea how to write one. Still, I gathered all my thoughts and began to write.

My very dear Sainu,
I have reached safely. I couldn't even write a letter because I was very busy with work. I know you must be worried. Don't worry. Your ikka is comfortable here. I am in a big firm that produces milk and wool. It is a good job. We don't need to do anything. The

machines take care of everything. I supervise the work
around here. My arbab likes me very much. He likes
my work, and often gives me presents. I stay in a very
expensive place. Sitting on my cot, I can see everything
that's around us. It is so beautiful. Ah, the food. How
many new and unseen items the arbab brings for
me! I started writing this letter after eating khubus
with chicken curry and mutton masala, and a glass
of pure milk. Indeed, I wonder if I have become fat
even within these few days! Now it is afternoon—rest
time. I need to get back to work after some time. Till
then, I can sleep in this pleasant breeze.

Some of our local people are here with me:
Ravuthar, Raghavan, Vijayan, Pokkar, and so on. I
do not interact with them much—the arbab doesn't
like it. The arbab has a houri of a daughter. Every
evening, she and I go for a stroll. She insists that I
must go with her. Her name is Marymaimuna.

This is my news. I hope you and Ummah are fine.
I shall write again when I get time.

Your own ikka,
Najeeb

I folded the paper. Closed my eyes. Wept for some
time. The truth was not in that letter, but in my tears.
Nobody read the truth.

Twenty

One evening, as I was walking with the goats, I noticed the eastern corner of the sky becoming dark and cloudy. I had observed the desert over the previous days. Usually the change of seasons was accompanied by a dust storm. By the time the dust storm disappeared, the weather would also have changed. In the desert, all changes were sudden; nothing was ever slow. The previous day might be very hot, but the next day might dawn chilly; it might be shivering cold one day and burning hot the next. One moment the sky would be pure without a speck of dust, but the next second a dust storm would churn that purity away. This storm too appeared in a similar fashion. The whole day had been fiery hot and all of a sudden a host of black clouds appeared in one corner of the sky. Within seconds the darkness flowed across the whole sky and blanketed the earth. A cold wind blew, slicing through my mind and body. I felt like I

had been thrown from the desert into the South Pole.
As if caught in a frenzy, the goats bounced around
aimlessly. A similar feeling overtook me. I was filled
with ecstasy. Leaving the goats to wander, I spread
my arms and sauntered through that chill.

It was only when the arbab came in his vehicle
and admonished me that I gathered the goats and
returned to the masara. By the time I reached the
masara, it had started drizzling. When the first drop
fell on me, I writhed like I had been stabbed. By my
calculation, it had been eight or ten months since a
drop of water touched my skin. The experience was
incredibly painful. Soon, it began to rain. And as each
drop fell on me, I felt like my body was being pierced.
Unable to stand that excruciating pain, I ran to cover
myself with a blanket. And it was not just me, even
the goats suffered. They began to bleat, emitting a
strange sound. The usually unruffled camels returned
in the rain looking troubled and hurt.

Along with the rain came thunder and lightning.
It seemed to me that lightning would strike and burn
out the whole masara.

Every time a raindrop fell on my head, my hair
stood on its end and trembled. My body alternately
burnt and shivered. I longed to get wet in the rain and

bathe. But I couldn't bear it. When I could take it no longer I ran to the arbab's tent. The sight I saw! The arbab crouched in a corner like a coward. More than anything else in the world, the arbab feared water, I felt. Nowhere had I ever come across so frightened a man. The arbab seemed to fear water falling on his body, as though it were the touch of a jinni. As the rain droplets blew into the tent, the arbab retreated even farther into the corner. I thought the arbab had probably not had a bath even once in his life.

In an unprecedented gesture, the arbab invited me into the tent. When I tried to sit on the floor, he made me sit on the cot. Like a frightened child, he grabbed my hand and then slithered under a blanket to screen the sight of the rain. Sitting in that posture, my hand touched something under the pillow. Cautiously, I tried to feel it again. It was the arbab's gun! Slowly, I pulled it out. The arbab did not notice, he was chanting 'ya Allah, ya Allah' and praying for the rain to stop.

A kind of wildness came over me. Just aim and pull the trigger and you will be saved. There is a vehicle outside with the key hanging from the ignition. You can find the road and escape somehow. This is the chance, the moment Allah the merciful has ordained for you to escape. If you do not use this moment, you might never get a chance like this, ever. You do know that such opportunities do not come again and again. Do it. Escape from this hell somehow. My hand indeed moved towards the trigger.

Suddenly the arbab started praying loudly, 'My Allah . . . you kept us safe. Had Najeeb not been here, I would have died of fear now.' That was the first time that the arbab said my name. I had even doubted that he knew my name. He usually called me 'himar' or '*inti*'. That call of prayer softened my heart. I didn't feel like escaping after killing a coward who had been crying for my help. I returned the gun to its place.

I felt very hot inside the tent, so I removed my wet sheet and released the arbab's hand. I threw away the wet clothes and bravely walked into the rain. Initially, my body pulsated with pain, as if it were being stabbed by several arrows. I endured it, and the pain gradually faded away. After that each raindrop refreshed me. I enjoyed that rain. Like lambs that can sense the coming of rain, I leapt around. And thus, after a very long time, the rain washed me clean. Dirt quietly trickled down my body.

At some point in the night, as the rain eased, the arbab ran out of the tent and drove away in his vehicle.

The other arbab did not come that night. After a while, the rain grew heavy again. That whole night, I was free, out of anyone's coercion or control. That night I could have run away. But I didn't go anywhere. As always, I didn't know where to go to reach a safe destination. So I gave up the desire to escape. How many such opportunities to escape do we give up every day? We who throw away the golden bowl of opportunities when it comes into our hand.

That night, I felt the need to do something. Something that violated captivity, something that would have annoyed the arbab. If I didn't do anything, it would have been a waste of those precious moments of freedom. The desire blossomed instantaneously: I must go up to the neighbouring masara, I must see my Hakeem. He was dropped there the night we arrived in this country, and he has not been seen since. I did not even know whether he was alive or dead or if he had escaped. The poor boy was so near, yet so far. It was only then that I registered the extent of my cocooned existence. Once or twice I had asked the arbab about Hakeem, but he had ignored the question as if he hadn't heard it at all. In that downpour, I walked towards Hakeem's masara. Apprehensively I knocked on the gate fastened with an iron padlock. I feared that I would be in trouble if there were arbabs present. Still, I called out. 'Hakeem, Hakeem, can you hear me? This is me, Najeeb . . . the Najeeb who had come to the Gulf with you . . . Are you there?'

There was no reply despite my incessant knocking. I was about to walk back disheartened when I saw a shadow moving far away. I called out loudly. 'Hakeem! Is that you? It's Najeeb.' I was afraid the rain's snake-whistle would drown my voice.

But I saw the shadowy figure slowly walk towards me.

'Hakeem, is that you? Come closer, it is me, Najeeb.'

When that figure came near me, I looked at it carefully. Dark, skinny, dishevelled, ugly. Another scary figure. This was not my Hakeem. He did not look like Hakeem. Hakeem was handsome. Very fair. Very good to look at. Strong for his age. I had even advised him in jest to stay put in Bombay and try his luck in Hindi films.

'Is there someone called Hakeem here? He is a friend of mine. He came along with me. I haven't seen him since then. Do you know him, or where he is?' In one breath, I bombarded the scary figure with questions as he walked towards me.

For some time, the hideous figure stared from the other side of the gate, as if I were speaking in a strange language. Then, quite unexpectedly, he hit his head against the gate and started crying. I got scared. Then, between sobs, came his heart-wrenching cry, 'My Najeeb ikka.' It was only then, only then, that I recognized Hakeem. Alarmed, I understood how circumstances could redraw a man's shape beyond recognition. I could estimate how the same circumstances must have changed me too—completely. I had not looked in a mirror since I had entered the desert. If I had, I might not have been able to recognize myself as well.

He cried a lot, recalling his ummah, uppah, relatives and Allah. I had no answers for him. I only had the strength to cry with him, holding his hands to my chest through the iron railings. The night washed away in tears.

Twenty-one

It rained for two more days. The masara was filthy and full of muck by the time it stopped. The foul smell of goat droppings, urine, decaying hay and grass rent the air. It took me three or four days of back-breaking work to clean it all up.

Then the desert's vaults were flung open for the winter. It was foggy and cold in the mornings. When I got up and looked around, all I could see was the white film of winter. Everything—the masara, the goats, the arbab, the tent—disappeared into that whiteness. It was only around nine o'clock that the fog faded and everything became visible again—though the hour is a guess on my part, for I was a lonely being with no sense of time—and, so, all routines were disrupted. During summer, the days were very long. The sun rose very early, by about three in the morning, and the light didn't fade till eight at night. But in the winter, the sun didn't rise till nine, and the light would fade just after lunch. By four it would be completely dark. So the hours one got to do work were limited. In the winter one had to finish work in about six to seven hours, the same work that took ten to fifteen hours in the summer. Moreover, it was hard to work properly because of the cold. Even at noon it was spine-piercingly cold. I could not even touch the water. My hands would become numb if I had to work with water. It was in those days that I learned that even cold water could burn skin. On one occasion, blisters appeared on my left palm as if it had been scalded with hot water, after it was in cold water for some time. I have heard that it is cold at the poles, but I don't know from where such cold comes to the desert!

I didn't have any special clothes to protect me from the cold. I only had that abaya, the long unwashed garment that the arbab had given me on my first day, which I never removed from my body. What I had was a woollen blanket left behind by the scary figure. I wore it during the first days of winter, but it was a bother. How could one run after goats and enter the masara to fill the containers with water or hay wearing a blanket? I gave it up. It became my habit to walk in the cold in that single piece of clothing.

Though I discovered it a little late, there was something that gave me heat even in the height of winter: sheep! It was a real comfort to walk among them. When the cold wind came whistling, I would hold the sheep close to my body. Whenever the cold pierced through the blanket to maul my body, I would go to the masara and lie there embracing the sheep. I spent the winter as a sheep among the sheep.

Apart from the raucous wind, another unwelcome guest came to the masara in winter: flies. There were flies all around. A thousand flies would sit on the khubus when it was taken out. One hand had to be free all the time to keep them away. If one went to the masara, one could hear them buzzing like wasps. Though I disliked those wretched flies, I began to think that they too had to live somewhere. And if they liked the masara the most, then let them live there!

*

That winter, had I wanted, I could have escaped along with Hakeem, taking cover in the heavy mist. But the same doubt that I had on the first night of rain cast a spell on me, paralysing me from making my escape. Where to go? I did not know anything about this country, not even about the area I was in. In which direction—east, south, west or north—should I run to find a way out? Here, surely, I didn't have enough food, water, clothes, a proper place to sleep, wages, dreams or aspirations. But I did have something precious left—my life! I had at least managed to sustain that. If I ran away into an unfamiliar desert I might lose even that. Then what would be the meaning of all that I had endured so far?

Every prison has its own aura of safety. I didn't feel up to bursting that bubble of security. I decided to wait for the appropriate opportunity to strike—when I was sure of reaching a safe location. Was my decision correct? I didn't know.

*

At the beginning of winter more sheep had been offloaded in the masara by trucks. It was their breeding time, the six months till summer. Actually, sheep survive best in cold, mountainous climates. Rearing them in the desert is an injustice to them. The desert is congenial to goats as they can endure the high temperatures. The arbab kept the sheep because of the profit he made from selling their wool. Although three-quarters would be sold by the time summer came, the ones that remained, suffered. As the temperature soared, they died sweltering in their own woollen coat. I witnessed this many times. The arbab didn't throw away any of the corpses. He'd drag them into his vehicle and drive away. They must have been served as fresh mutton in some restaurant or the other later.

One day, when the winter was coming to an end, two men came to shear the sheep. They were Sudanese and both of them had broad smiles. Filled with the joy of meeting people after a long time, I followed them around like a puppy. But they didn't understand much of what I said and neither did I make sense of what they said. But it was with broad smiles that they remained uncomprehending of my words.

That year the Sudanese came with a machine to shear wool and a generator to work it; previously they had used hand-held scissors. The arbab began to jump around like a troubled jinni as soon as they started the generator and the machine. His first fear was that his sheep would get electrocuted. The poor men had to struggle to convince the arbab that the machine wouldn't kill the sheep with electric shocks. The arbab's second fear was that the machine would shear more wool than necessary and the sheep would burn to death in summer. (There would be no demand for such sheep in the market.) It was only after they had demonstrated on a sheep that the machine was set to shear only to a certain thickness that the arbab half-heartedly gave his consent. Even then he continued to express his displeasure at the use of the machine.

It was my duty to secure the sheep for shearing. I had to do that after carrying out all my daily chores. I held the sheep by their necks between my knees, like I had the kids that were castrated. It took hardly a minute or two to finish shearing one sheep, but it was a back-breaking job for me to hold some six hundred of them like that over two days. The machine would shear the sheep bare, only leaving some wool on its tail. 'This is how we shear in our land. The tail hair is our gift to the sheep to swat flies,' the Sudanese smiled, showing his white teeth.

All the sheep were shorn by the next afternoon and they looked like gorgeous lads and lasses. By evening, the Sudanese packed the wool in sacks and left in their pick-up. The sense of dejection that descended on me as they departed! I had been enjoying the scent of two humans till then. Now, there were only the animals and me. Grief came, like rain.

*

Winter was also the time when I learned that it was impossible to wipe out life on this earth whatever man's misdeeds. For how many months had this desert been lying under scorching heat! There had been no sign of life on those burning sands. As the cold wind blew, signalling summer's end, a green carpet surfaced on the dry sand. This was within two days of the rain! It was as if all the scents of life had been lying dormant beneath that brown surface, straining to hear the music of resurrection: cactuses, creepers, rock fungi, touch-me-nots, bushes with shiny leaves. And from the ends of the sky came flocks of birds that spread their long wings, warbling swallows, chattering green parrots, pairs of cooing doves. Where did they all come from?

The realization that those plants and animals had been lying quietly—preserving their lives, withstanding the heat of the desert—filled me with delight. I saw with my own eyes how those little plants grew big, bore flowers and fruit, and concealed life for the future in the womb of the earth. How much I admired them! Those plants taught me life's great lessons of hope. They whispered to me: Najeeb, adopted son of the desert, like us, you too must preserve your life and wrestle with this desert. Hot winds and scorching days will pass. Don't surrender to them. Don't grow weary, or you might have to pay with your life. Don't give in. Lie half dead, as if meditating. Feign nothingness. Convey the impression that you will never resurrect. Secretly appeal to Allah the merciful. He will recognize your presence. He will hear your cries. And finally an opportune moment will come for you. This hot wind will blow away. This heat will dissipate. The cold wind of time will beckon you. Then, only then, should you slowly raise your head from the earth, announce your presence and, then, quickly, spring to freedom. Bloom and come to fruit in the morrow.

I lent my ears to the words of the little plants. I waited patiently for the opportune moment.

Twenty-two

Although I feared and hated the male goats, there was also an instance when one of them happened to save my life. One day, I took them for a walk as usual. Leaving them to wander, I climbed up and sat on a sand dune. I don't know why, memories of homeland awakened in me. All my suppressed thoughts stirred and erupted like a volcano. I must escape from here. I must go home. I must reach my ummah. I must see my Sainu. I must see my Nabeel. I must see my land. I must see my dusty roads. I must see my river. I must see my canoe. I must see my rain. I must see my earth. At such moments, I could truly comprehend the meaning of nostalgia. It is a craving. An acute craving that makes us hate our present condition. Then, that craving takes the form of a crazy urge to rush home, like a wild boar rushing wildly through sugarcane fields when it's been shot. It happens only once in a while. But when it does, it is not easy to shut down the surge of emotions.

The arbab was standing up on his vehicle with his binoculars. As I was sitting on the other side of the sand dune, for the time being, I was outside the binoculars' range. I took this as an opportunity to escape. I told myself that I would be doomed to this life if I hesitated. I jumped up as if on Allah's invitation. I thought of nothing else and bolted through the desert. Alas, a billy goat that was standing near me also began to run alongside. Although I tried to dissuade it, hitting and poking it with my staff, it kept following me. Because of my extreme desire to escape, I did not look back at all. Far off, as far as possible, that was all my mind was saying. I had no idea where I was going. Just run, just escape, that's all, I kept telling myself. The goat was just behind me, and it was running as if it would gore me down. Fearing that, I doubled my speed.

Suddenly, I heard the roar of a vehicle behind me. Fear blazed inside me like fire. The arbab had seen me running! The arbab would reach me soon and he would beat me to death. All of a sudden, a gunshot rang out. Fortunately, it did not hit me. Although I knew I would not make it, I kept running, trying to go faster. As soon as the second shot was fired, the goat came flying towards me with a loud cry and rolled over me. Blood gushed out of its chest, as if from a motor pump. Writhing in pain, it leapt up and ran. After a short distance, worn out, it fell down. By then, the arbab had reached me. I ran and fell at his feet. The arbab removed his belt and whipped me. I howled. The arbab commanded me to get into the vehicle. Like a smacked puppy whining and running into its kennel with its tail between its legs, I ran and got into the back of the arbab's pick-up. The goat was dead by then. The arbab dragged it and flung it into the vehicle and gave me another smack. Downcast, I sat there and wailed.

Open-eyed, the corpse of the goat lay next to me. My sobs became intense as I realized that it had died because of me. My dear goat . . . who asked you to come after me? To show your breast to the bullet that was ordained for me? My feeling that it was time to escape was wide of the mark. I had wrongly judged Allah's call. Often it is like that; we justify our desires as the call of Allah. But things happen only according to Allah's will. To discern his will correctly, one has to be close to Allah. I hadn't anticipated the signs. But Allah had protected me. Were you sacrificed instead of me? Like the goat that was sacrificed instead of the son of Prophet Ibrahim?

The vehicle stopped in front of the tent. The arbab dragged me out and locked me up in a masara after tying me up. Then he beat me to his heart's content. Blood oozed from all parts of my body. Still, I didn't cry. I didn't shed a tear. I endured everything. A goat gave up its life for me. If I cry about my fate, even Allah will not forgive me.

The arbab skinned the goat right there. He chopped it into pieces and roasted it a fire in the open. He ate to his fill and brought the rest to me. When I declined, he hit me some more and forced the meat into my mouth and made me eat it. I felt nauseated, as if I was devouring my own brother's flesh. I couldn't eat any of it. I vomited the little that went in. Since then I have never eaten mutton. I have never felt like having it.

The arbab left me locked up in the masara that day and the next. He didn't let me out at all, didn't even give me a drop of water or a piece of khubus. For two days, I lay there without complaint. By the second night, I was very hungry. When I was sure that the arbab was asleep, I slowly untied my legs and, creeping out through the goats, I reached the water container and drank water till my thirst was quenched. In the next container, there were some wheat grains left uneaten by the goats. I gathered them up and ate greedily. Raw wheat. Unhusked. There was some salt in the small pail nearby. I ate the wheat with the salt. It was on that day that I realized uncooked wheat could be tasty! I guzzled water again from the container. My belly full, I was finally at ease. I slept in the masara with the goats.

By then I had indeed become a goat.

Twenty-three

Even though summer had set in the heat was tolerable. But as I found out later that was just the beginning of the season. As the days passed, the temperature rose steadily. Heat filled the air in all its intensity. Each time the wind blew, I felt like I was inside a furnace.

What do you think I wanted most during my first summer in the desert? Freedom? Water? Good food? Seeing my child? Calling my Sainu once? No, none of those. My fervent desire was to sit in a bit of shade for some time. You can imagine my sufferings if *that* was what I dreamt of and longed for! I tried to make some shade with my garment. I even tried to find some shade in the shadow that fell from my staff. I had only heard about places that didn't have shadows even the size of a crow's wing. It was in the desert I experienced its reality.

This summer, however, I managed to make a tent by spreading the woollen blanket over my cot. When I sat under it, the heat was somewhat bearable. But I hardly found the time to relax. Work started at five in the morning. It wasn't done even by ten at night. When I returned with the goats from one section of the masara, the arbab would have released the goats from the next. I just had time to drink two mugs of water—water that had been literally boiling in the rusty iron tank! By then the goats would be spreading out in the desert and if I didn't get them together, they would go their separate ways. Gathering them after that would be impossible. I'd run to them without wasting a minute at the masara, frothing at the mouth like a rabid dog.

I would raise my eyes to the heavens and ask, my Allah, what crime have I committed against you and my father to be left to wander with animals in this desert like the prodigal son? Allah would look back at me in the shape of the burning sun. He would tell me, the days of suffering you must go through are not over yet. Like a prophet in the desert, I would kneel on the hot sand and pray looking at the sky: My Allah, release me from this affliction. Send me a saviour as you sent Moses to the Israelites. Liberate me from this captivity.

I didn't know if Allah heard me or not. But the belief that Allah was looking after me instilled in me a new confidence. Non-believers, those of you fortunate to live merrily in the pleasant greenery Allah has bestowed on you, you might feel prayers are ridiculous rituals. For me, prayers were my bolt-hole. It was because of faith alone that I could be strong in spirit even when I was weak in my body. Otherwise I would have withered and burnt like grass in that blazing wind.

The sand cools faster than it warms up. By eight or nine in the night, the sand would be cold. Then, it was pleasant to sleep on the sand. It was as if a spring had sprouted from the earth's interior, cooling the sand and me on top of it. Ah, how pleasant it was! It would wash away the entire day's fatigue. I refuse to believe that the earth's interior is boiling hot. I also won't believe that there is no water in the desert. I am certain that there was a river flowing silently under the sandy plain I lay on. I slept on that flow, like on a raft. Even thinking about that experience doubles my contentment and sleep now. However, my peace of mind did not last long. It ended on a note of fear. I will tell you why.

One morning, when I entered the masara, I saw four or five goats lying dead on the ground. I was frightened.

They had been leaping about yesterday without any problems. One of them was about to give birth. I could not figure out what had happened. Could it be some disease that struck them? Allah, is it some kind of contagious disease? If so, wouldn't I have detected some symptoms? Nervously, I ran towards the arbab's tent. I told him what had happened. In Malayalam. The arbab must have learned my language by then. Even otherwise, hasn't it been proven many times that if necessity demands, a listener can understand any language. But it is also my experience that whatever the language, the listener will never understand if the need of the speaker to communicate is greater than the listener's to understand.

The arbab got up and walked with me to the masara; he circled the dead goats, turned them over and inspected them. Opened their eyelids and looked into them. I waited, expecting to be accused and beaten. But nothing happened. The arbab walked around the masara looking for clues. Then he brought a shovel from the pick-up and asked me to dig a pit. When I finished digging, the arbab dragged the goats and dumped them in it. I was very surprised. Would my arbab, who wouldn't even spare salt to apply on a wound, let so much mutton go waste? I just did not understand, neither did he explain. I returned to my routine.

I milked the goats and served some milk to the arbab, drank some myself and gave the rest to the lambs. I went out with the goats, came back and ate two khubus, cleaned the masara, and filled all the different containers. My chores did not stop. What did it matter to me if the goats were dead or alive? It was only the arbab's loss. I didn't have anything to gain or lose. Still, a pain lingered throughout the day like soreness from an insect sting. Despite my best efforts to remain composed, those deaths kept haunting me. Especially the death of the pregnant goat. That goat was going to give birth for the first time! I could see its pride in all its movements and looks. Even though it was a goat, it too must have had dreams. How many times must it have dreamt about becoming a mother, feeding its child and playing with it? Poor thing, all of it ended in one night. That is life.

Goat, my dear goat, your life and mine are someone else's gift. Neither you nor I have any right to live even a day more than we are permitted to by He who gifted it to us. We can't escape from this world without going through all that we are destined to endure. Goat, your stars were unlucky, you were condemned to die before you could even look at your child. I am twice as doomed. I too must go through hell in this masara. I too haven't even seen my child. What a wretched life!

At night, after my meal of khubus, I lay down on the bare sand, with a stone for a pillow.

To my surprise, the arbab started his vehicle. A hope rose in me that he might leave for while. If so, I must abscond. I lay down as if I hadn't noticed him. But all my senses were keenly alert. The arbab began driving around the masara. Very slowly, as if he was searching for something. After four or five rounds, he returned to the tent and stopped the car. Then he went inside the tent. Within an instant, all the stars rising towards hope were doused in darkness. I was angry and frustrated. I cursed everything. I even cursed Allah.

The arbab drove around the masara many more times that night. I didn't understand why he was doing that, nor did I ask. After all, goats do not talk to men.

Lying in sandy comfort, I slept. It must have been late at night when I woke up to the commotion of goats bleating and milling about. When I looked around, I saw the arbab panicking and running around the iron fence. He was also calling me, '*Hayya, hayya . . .*' I jumped up and went to his side. The arbab gave me a stick and pushed me into the masara. Completely at a loss, I stood there as the arbab started his vehicle to illuminate the place. The goats continued to bleat. Slowly, moving aside each goat, I looked for what was disturbing them. Finally, I caught sight of the reason why the goats were so jumpy. A snake! A snake coiled around a goat's leg. I ran out, crying in fear.

At home, I wouldn't even go in the direction where a mud snake or a water snake had been sighted, for three days at least. Even the mention of a snake terrified me. Seeing me so frightened, the arbab came out angrily and pushed me back inside and locked the masara from outside. Now I had only two options. Either kill the snake or die of snakebite. Necessity bestows a man with courage he did not know he possessed. I had many unfulfilled aspirations throbbing inside me, so I had to be bold. To live was my necessity.

Tiptoeing, I aimed for the leg of the goat on which the snake had coiled itself. It is very difficult to kill a snake in a crowd of people or goats. The stick merely touched its body when it turned towards me, hissing. I ran out. But the masara door was locked. Mad with fear, I started hitting out left and right. Most of the blows landed on the backs of the goats. They began to run around but I kept on hitting. None of the strikes landed on the snake. But it must have got frightened by the sound of the blows because it went away on its own.

I was heavily reprimanded by the arbab. One of the goats died from my blows. I lost my peace of mind that night. I also lost the pleasure of sleeping on the cool sand. For how many days had I been sleeping on the ground exposed to the mercy of the poisonous snake? It could have slithered towards me, bitten me and killed me. I had heard that desert snakes were very poisonous. A mere touch is enough to end a life. But no snakes had come for me in all the days I slept on the ground. They must have moved away, knowing that I was sleeping there. Allah the merciful decides everything in advance. Everything happened only according to His plans. Not even a snake bit against His wish. Allah, praise be to you!

The next morning, three young goats were found dead in the masara. One of them was my Nabeel.

Twenty-four

If I am asked about the most beautiful sight I ever saw in the desert, I must answer: the sunset. The sun seems like a tortoise diving down into the sand. Slowly, it sinks into the sandy jungle. I often wished that Sainu was with me to watch the sunset. Although I said that I tried to keep memories of my home, homeland and Sainu at bay, she appeared in my thoughts on such occasions. My heart would then throb. One of the greatest sorrows in the world is to not have someone to share a beautiful sight. I drew my eyes away from sunset and lay on my back on the cot. Like an orphan's corpse . . .

That night I went to sleep under a star-studded sky. But when I woke up the air was filled with dust though there was no sign of a wind. Dust had sneaked in from somewhere and filled the air. I felt like laughing when I looked at my body. Like a comedian in some movie, my whole body was covered in scales of dust.

I looked at the goats; they too were painted in the colour of dust. The buckets in the masara, the iron fence, the camels, the arbab's tent, the vehicle, my cot, the bundles of hay—dust covered everything. It brought to mind film scenes showing snowfall in cold countries.

I shook my head and dust enough for a brick kiln fell out of my hair. And when I tried to run my fingers through my hair, it was so matted with sand and dirt that my fingers couldn't get inside. My hair was already shoulder length. My beard had also grown. I took the big sheep-shearing scissors and manically cut away at my hair and beard. I got a wild itch from the unwashed hair and beard sometimes. I already had blisters from the dirty hair in my armpits and pubic area and had become revolting to look at. Lice, bugs and some other small insects from the goats' bodies had settled there. They itched severely when I sweated at night. My body had become a pest reserve. Lice and bugs formed a crust on my skin. The goats were cleaner than I was.

Twenty-five

Hadn't I promised to tell you the story of Pochakkari Ramani? And I will now. Apart from Pochakkari Ramani, I gave a name to each goat in the masara that I recognized to help me scold them and to make cuddling easier. People from my locality like Aravu Ravuthar, Marymaimuna, Indipokkar, Njandu Raghavan, Parippu Vijayan, Chakki, Ammini, Kausu, Raufat, Pinki, Ammu, Razia and Thahira, and public figures like Jagathy, Mohanlal and even EMS himself were a part of my masara. Each of them was dear to me in one way or another. Have you ever looked carefully at a goat's face? It is quite similar to a human's. I named the goats not only by looking at their faces but also relating their names to some character traits, their gait, the sounds they made, by incidents that reminded me of them. Just as how one gets a nickname back home.

I have told you about the billy goat who attacked me and broke my hand. I called him Aravu Ravuthar after the rowdiest person in our village. One day, my uppah was crossing a stream on a narrow bridge. Ravuthar approached from the other side. The bridge was so narrow that only one person could walk on it, that too barely. Unmindful that my uppah had already crossed half the bridge, Ravuthar walked up to him and asked him to retreat. Uppah didn't want to. Ravuthar warned him once, and when my uppah didn't move even after the second warning, he didn't bother to repeat himself, he just leapt and head-butted uppah on his chest! Uppah fell down into the stream some twelve feet below. His elbow hit a granite rock and he broke his arm. Although he was taken to Alappuzha District Hospital immediately for treatment, his hand remained weak and crooked. Thus did my uppah get the nickname short-arm Abdu. I named the goat Aravu Ravuthar without much difficulty because he butted me in the same manner as I imagine the original Aravu Ravuthar must have attacked my uppah. Also, my hand broke just like my uppah's did.

So there were many strange and personal reasons for each name I gave the goats. The logic of the names might be lost on others but they made perfect sense to me.

The name Marymaimuna too had such a story. Mary was the first heroine of my love story. My first love affair began when I was studying in the fifth standard. She was the most intelligent and beautiful girl I ever knew, and a wonderful singer. There were no boundaries for the dreams I had about her. Somehow, my ummah found out. That tactical deceiver—my elder ikka Abdu—who managed to get me to tell him my secret must have told her. Bouncing her big breasts, my ummah laughed on hearing about it.

'By the sound of her name she seems to be a Christian,' Ummah frowned between peals of laughter.

'No, Ummah, she belongs to our religion,' I broke in excitedly.

'A Mary in our religion?' Ummah laughed aloud.

It was only then that I actually gave her religion some thought—that she might not belong to our religion at all. 'She's not Mary, Ummah,' I told her a name that came to my mind, 'she's Marymaimuna.'

'All right. I am coming to your school. I want to see the girl with that name,' Ummah continued laughing.

My ummah couldn't come to school to see my Marymaimuna. I stopped going to school before she could. That was the year my father died.

It was a name that I had completely forgotten. Marymaimuna. But when I saw a particularly beautiful goat in the masara, in tremendous waves all those memories rushed back to me. To me, that goat had the same beauty as Marymaimuna!

Would you believe me if I told you that in my masara we had goats that laughed like Jagathy, walked like Mohanlal, stammered like EMS? Only a few goats were permanent residents in the masara: the female goats that produced babies constantly and gave enough milk, and some virile male goats. All the remaining ones were dispatched to the market at some point or the other. The most interesting thing was that when one with a particular name went away, that name did not die out. After some time, a goat with similar qualities appeared. Then I repeated the names: Jagathy, Mohanlal, Njandu Raghavan, Kausu, Ammini . . . I think that, for both men and goats, births are but reincarnations from generation to generation.

I started calling the goat whom I approached first when I was deputed to milk Pochakkari Ramani. It was the goat whose udders I touched for the first time. That name's relevance lies in an incident that happened when I was young. One of my uncles, Pokkar mama, used to visit our house frequently. Whenever he came to visit us, he took me out for a walk in the afternoon. Before we stepped out, he would say to my ummah, 'Atha, give me twenty-five paise to buy him sweets.' And every time, Ummah gave him twenty-five paise, but I never got any sweets. Not only that, Pokkar mama only took me to the field nearby. We would wait there for the women to come and cut grass. Ramani was one of the many women who came to cut grass. It was Mama's routine to pay Ramani the money he got from ummah to buy me sweets so that he could fondle her breasts.

I too developed a desire to fondle her breasts! 'You can also fondle my breasts if you bring me twenty-five paise,' Pochakkari Ramani said. She gave me a knock on my head and chased me away when I told her that I didn't have any money. At home I was afraid to ask for money. I would only get a beating. Still, I had to fondle those breasts. So I pinched twenty-five paise from Ummah's rice box. Thus, one day, to my delight, I too got to fondle the fodder girl Ramani's breasts and enjoy the experience. But Ummah, who kept an account of every paisa, caught my theft. I divulged the truth when she questioned me. Pokkar mama's visits to our house stopped after that incident and he got the nickname 'breast mama'. Pochakkari Ramani eventually became a well-known prostitute in our locality!

Twenty-six

We can endure any misery if we have someone to share it with. Being lonely is very depressing. Words twitched like silverfish inside me. Unshared emotions pulsated, bubbled and frothed at my mouth. An ear to pour out my sorrows, two eyes to look at me and a cheek beside me became essential for my survival. In their absence one turns mad, even suicidal. It might be the reason why people condemned to solitary confinement turn insane.

Getting those words out, expelling them, provides the greatest mental peace. Those who do not get this chance die choking on words. I too would have died like that. But it was through the stories I narrated to my Pochakkari Ramani, my Marymaimuna, my Kausu and Aravu Ravuthar that I threw out those words accumulating inside me. I kept talking to them as if I were talking to dear ones when I walked them, milked them, filled their containers and gave them fodder. I poured out my tears, pains, sufferings, emotions and dreams. I do not know if they understood anything. But they listened to me, looked at me with raised eyes, even shed tears with me. That was enough for me.

In those days when I had only goats for company, there was an occasion when I shared with them not only my sorrows and pains, but also my body. One night, as I lay down, I could not sleep. I didn't know why, but I was covered in sweat. I had an insatiable desire, a passion building up inside me like a desert storm. For some time, I had been impotent. I did not think I would have the urge to be sexually active again. But it happened. What had lain dormant for so long suddenly woke up. All my efforts to satiate it only made me crave it even more. Seductive nude female figures began to slither in front of my eyes. I thawed in that emotional surge. I needed a body to lie close to. I needed a cave to run into. I became mad. In the intensity of that madness, I got up and rushed out. When I opened my tired eyes in the morning, I was in the masara. With Pochakkari Ramani lying close to me.

*

The desire to see Hakeem again also increased after I learned that he was in the neighbouring masara. My eyes had this craving to see another human being. He was also searching for ways to meet me. We realized that we had not run into each other in the desert till then because we had been taking our goats in different directions. Between our two masaras, there was a small valley. It ruined all the chances of our meeting. Slowly, however, I started going towards that valley. I began to spot Hakeem at a distance. He too started moving towards me. We began to meet though the arbab often scolded me about it. But I didn't heed his words. My fear of him had vanished through constant exposure to it. What would happen? Some rebuke, some smacks. I had got used to both.

Hakeem's arbab was worse than mine. Sometimes he told me about the torment he had to undergo. His arbab's pastime included flicking boiling water on Hakeem's face, pulling his hair, poking a stick into his backside, kicking his chest, dunking his head in water, etc. Therefore Hakeem was very afraid of our meetings being detected by his arbab. On the occasions when he actually came, he would run away after saying a word or two. We even devised ways to meet each other. For that, I would poke a stick into a goat's anus or twist its tail. Then the goat would run crazily. I would run after it and hit it, which would make it run even faster. Thus, somehow, I would get near Hakeem. When the arbab looked from afar through his binoculars, it appeared as though I had reached the place chasing a runaway goat. We would quickly exchange a word or two. Our conversation would end there. It had to end there. If we spent even a little more time, the arbab would arrive in his vehicle. Just imagine how much we had to restrain ourselves to squeeze in all our thoughts into two pairs of words. A person who has the opportunity to talk incessantly all through the day would not be able to easily relate to my torment.

Twenty-seven

One day, I was sitting on a sand dune, watching over the goats. I could see Hakeem with his goats in the distance. I thought about going up to him for a chat. But the arbab hadn't taken his eyes off the binoculars. His supervision had increased in the past few days. He had in fact strictly forbidden me from meeting Hakeem. It could be that he feared our frequent meetings might kindle in us a desire to escape together. But the reason my arbab gave me was different—that there might be germs and diseases in the other masara which could spread to our masara and to our goats through my contact with Hakeem. To tell you the truth, I felt like laughing—as if my masara was the abode of hygiene!

Anyway, I suppressed my desire to talk to Hakeem. I could somehow bear with the beatings and scoldings, but why should I push Hakeem towards the same fate?

Maybe because of that distant view of Hakeem, suddenly I was struck by the thoughts of the homeland. It did not happen very often during my life in the masara. All my longings rose in unison inside me. My Sainu, my ummah, my son . . . my daughter . . .? My house, my canoe. How many times had I heard about the nostalgia of the diaspora? It often surprised me later that I never grieved for my shattered dreams even in those hostile situations. I think such thoughts come only to those who can see an exit. I never thought that I would escape from the hell I was in. Once trapped, I carried on living with no hopes of escape. The dead don't dream about life. But that day, a faint hope that I might also escape sprouted in me.

Merciful Allah, you perform great miracles in the lives of many: a beggar strikes gold by winning a jackpot, a sick man regains his health one fine morning, the victim of an accident leaves the place without a scratch, one person escapes while hundred others perish in a plane crash, a shipwrecked sailor makes it to the shore, someone comes up alive weeks later from the ruins of an earthquake. How many such events challenge common sense? Won't you make such a miracle happen in my life? You just need to will it. What if a hay truck driver stopped his vehicle for me? A water truck man transported me to a safe place? Why, what if the arbab himself took pity on me and sent me back? Your will alone is required, your benevolence. I looked at the heavens. There were pale clouds floating like orphans, showing me no sign of hope.

It was then that I saw two billy goats locking horns. When these goats locked horns with each other, they turned twice as aggressive. They would stop only when their horns would break and heads bleed. The fury one male had towards another! I ran towards them and hit them. Seething with anger, one moved away. The other turned towards me and breathed fire from his nostrils, locking his eyes with mine. He drew all his fury to his horns. I didn't budge from where I stood. As he leapt at me, I evaded him quickly. I had learned the manoeuvre from experience. A goat would never attack abruptly. It would stop, take aim and then leap. Until then, one should remain still. Dive away as it charges towards you. With the momentum carrying it forward, it can't change direction. That's the only way to dodge the charge of a billy goat.

As the goat lost its target, it nosedived into the ground. The fall took away its fury. Somehow it got up and went away in another direction. The goat's fall had made a depression in the sand. When I looked there casually, I thought I spotted something. There was some evidence of previous digging. Tense, I walked up to the spot. The sight stunned me. I glanced at the arbab. He was resting, his eyes off the binoculars. I sat down and began to dig slowly. My suspicion came true. I jumped up horrified when I saw it. It was a human palm! A palm rotting away to the bones. With intense fear and anxiety I started brushing away the sand. I had merely removed a layer of the earth when a human skeleton came into view. I was really terrified now. As I stepped back, something struck my foot. A leather belt that had not yet decomposed. A belt that looked familiar. Suddenly, lightning struck me. I had seen that belt on the waist of the scary figure who had disappeared from the masara the third day after I reached.

I bolted towards the masara, leaving the goats there. I went and fell at the feet of the arbab. 'I don't want to go anywhere. I am not going to abscond from this place. It is enough if you don't kill me. I don't even mind living like this. I am afraid of death.' I kept crying. The arbab was bemused. He couldn't figure out the reason for my sudden outburst!

Twenty-eight

Every experience in life has a climax, whether it be happiness, sorrow, sickness or hunger. When we reach the end, there are only two paths left for us: either we learn to live with our lives or protest and struggle in a final attempt to escape. If we choose the second path, we are safe if we win; if not, we end up in a mental asylum or kill ourselves.

So far I had not tried to escape. The first few times were amateurish attempts. I had not reached the end of my tether then. Actually, I had learnt to live with my circumstances. My experience taught me that no matter how severe our pain or how harsh the difficulties we face, we come to terms with our miseries in the course of time. I became used to my life over the course of a year. I no longer found it burdensome. In the past I used to wonder how beggars, the very poor, the permanently sick, the blind and the handicapped went on with their lives, how happy smiles broke out on their faces. Now I had my answer—from life itself. I didn't feel like my life had any difficulties any more. What did I have to do? Wake up in the morning, milk the goats, give fodder to the animals, take the goats for a walk, come back, eat khubus, go to bed in daylight and moonshine. No thoughts, no worries, no desires. What else did I need? I didn't know anything about what was happening in the outside world. I had forgotten my family, my home, my homeland. They had become to me people who had lived with me in some other life or time. I was not at all affected by their sorrows or their miseries. My life was happy. Happy.

Thus, in my life, summer came, winter came, wind came, dust storm came, rain came now and then, trucks came once a week. Everything came. Everything left. Only my goats and I stayed in the masara without leaving. And Hakeem and his goats in the neighbouring masara. It was then that an unfortunate third came into our midst. He was brought to Hakeem's masara. Hakeem and he were together all the time. That was the first time I envied another human being so deeply. In fact, I was morose. Hakeem had someone to talk to, to communicate with. I remained a goat in the masara of goats. I began to hate myself even more.

Twenty-nine

The changes in Hakeem were visible. I didn't know anything about the new arrival, who he was or where he came from. But he brought great changes in Hakeem's life. Large smiles broke out on his face. His words were joyful. I shrank into a shell out of sheer envy. I felt anger and animosity towards the whole world. I gave vent to my bitterness by taking it out on the goats in the masara—by squashing the balls of the newborn males, jabbing at the udders of the milk-goats with my staff, and shoving sticks up the ass of the sheep.

Initially Hakeem was timid about coming to the place where I herded the goats. But after he got a companion, he began to come there quite often. Although he didn't come very near, he came within shouting distance. Though his arbab hit him for making these forays, the boldness Hakeem acquired from his new companion made it possible to for him to keep coming. I really wanted to see his friend. But he didn't come out of the masara too often. While Hakeem took the goats outside, he did the chores inside the masara.

However, one day Hakeem brought him to meet me. He was a gigantic figure. Very tall. My first impression was that he seemed like a character from Prophet Musa's time. From a distance I was convinced that he was a Pathan from Pakistan. They came close and Hakeem introduced him to me: Ibrahim Khadiri from Somalia. A banyan tree that had grown in an African desert! Hakeem and I looked like wilting plants in front of that banyan tree. (Because of that meeting both saplings got enough beatings!)

Some time after that meeting, when we spotted each other in the desert, Hakeem climbed up a sand dune and shouted to me: 'I have left a note for you. Read it.' And he went away. After a while, I went with my goats towards the sand dune where he had stood. There, under a stone was a piece of paper. I read it.

Ibrahim Khadiri has been in this country before this. Knows all places and roads. Plans to abscond. Will take us too. Will let you know if anything materializes. Trust in Allah the merciful.

The joy that fizzed inside me! I cannot describe it in words! I was like a flower that was forced to blossom in the desert. It was a lie when I said I had not been thinking about my homeland and home. An outright lie. My every thought was occupied by fantasies of my homeland. I had only buried them underneath the cinders of my circumstances. I could see them come ablaze as soon as the wind of a chance blew. I felt my heart ache. A draining heartache. I cried. I hugged and gave Marymaimuna who was nearby a kiss. I am leaving, girl, leaving you. I am going. Don't you have many Aravu Ravuthars and Moori Vasus here to keep you company? I don't have anyone. My Sainu and I don't have anyone. I need her. And she needs me.

I prostrated myself on the ground. I thanked Allah the merciful for remembering me. For having heard my cries. For sending the prophet Ibrahim Khadiri to release me. Allahu Akbar! Allahu Akbar!

How joyful my day had become. How enthusiastically I completed every chore. The arbab must have wondered about the sudden change in me. Arbab, beware. Only a few more days. It's all going to be over. I will leave. Then let us see who you will spit at and beat with the belt. You will be alone. Then you will realize the value of this Najeeb.

I hoped my freedom would come soon. But nothing happened that day. I waited eagerly the next day. My anticipation was stronger on that day than the first. But nothing happened. There was expectation the day after that. But its intensity had diminished. Then, with every passing day, the tide of hope slowly began to ebb. It finally ended in terrible frustration. I despised myself and hated Ibrahim Khadiri and Hakeem for cheating me.

The hatred continued for two days. Then apprehension sneaked in. Had they escaped, deserting me? I couldn't even imagine such a thing. If that was the case, I even resolved to take revenge on them by committing suicide. It was with anxiety that I looked out for Hakeem every morning when I took the goats out. And I experienced an unexplainable tenderness towards them when I learned that they were still there. It was the tenderness arising from the acknowledgement that I was not alone.

Gradually, I began to blame my fate. It was sport for Allah to play with me, have people lie to me, torment me. There is Najeeb to undergo everything you can throw at him. Allah, you didn't have to do this to me.

In the next few days I began to lose all hope. There is no Khadiri-Podiri to redeem me. My fate is to live here and die here. My days went back to how they had been. With nothing to hope for. Nothing to dream about. A goat's life.

Thirty

It happened when I was least expecting it. Hakeem came to me driving a goat. 'Something's happening day after tomorrow. Be prepared!' He ran back after saying that. It was as if he had dropped burning embers in my mind. *Something*. What could it be? Still, he had asked me to be prepared. It was a good omen. But the fear that I experienced then! I suddenly lost all urge to escape. Even when it is set free, a goat reared in a cage will return to the cage. I had become like that. I can't go anywhere in this figure and form. I am a goat. My life is in this masara. Till I end my life or die of some disease, I don't want to show anyone this scruffy shape, this scruffy face, this scruffy life. Mine is a goat's life.

I had been waiting for this chance ever since I got here. But when the opportunity offered itself, I became detached. Life is full of strange contradictions. In those two days, I didn't make any preparations. Nor did I feel any special excitement. How many times had I readied my mind for such a chance to escape! But my fate felt like that of a bride whose groom ditched her on her wedding day. So I wasn't willing to raise my hopes. I even cursed Hakeem for trusting the words of that African crook Ibrahim Khadiri.

That evening, surprisingly, the arbab called me to his tent. He asked me to sit inside. I was amazed. 'Tonight is the wedding of the elder arbab's daughter. So neither of us will be here. Stay awake through the night and watch over the goats. A fox may come. Snakes may come. Even thieves. You should look after everything. When I return in the morning, I will bring you khubus, biryani and majbus. Okay? You are my trusted servant. I've never had a servant like you till now. All the others who had been here were lazy. You are good. I like you. May Allah protect you.'

I nodded my head and listened to everything. This was the opportunity Hakeem had alluded to! If so, today is that happy day. Like a butterfly's wing, my mind fluttered with joy. But I didn't betray any signs of it outside. Donning a disinterested air, I came out of the tent. Those words were the reward for all my hard labour till then. Yes, only those words. I hadn't got anything else.

At night someone else whom I had never seen before arrived in a vehicle. It was only when I saw the whiteness and cleanness of his dress that I noticed my own condition. Oh, how piteous I looked! I rated myself as the god of impurity.

When the visitor drove away taking my arbab with him, a strange enthusiasm possessed me, like the excitement of children left to play at home when their parents head off for a party. I ran around the masara in ecstasy. Shouting, laughing, leaping around. I ran towards Hakeem's masara. There was Hakeem, so joyful. As soon as he saw me he ran towards me. He hugged me. Kissed me. We hugged and cried. 'Ikka, I want to see my ummah. Want to see my uppah. Want to see my sister Shahina. I can't stand it any more, ikka,' he cried out in grief.

'Sure, dear. Everything that you want will happen. Didn't Allah bring us to this point? Just a few hours more. We have the Lord with us. Be brave,' I consoled him, patting his cheeks.

Ibrahim was sitting on a cot. 'Aren't we leaving?' I went up to him anxiously. Turning to me he smiled, revealing his gums. An innocent smile, like a baby's. 'Haven't you suffered for so long, Najeeb?' he rose up and touched my shoulder, 'Just wait a little longer. Let the arbabs reach where they are headed for. From where it takes a long time to return. Don't forget that we will be on foot. You should return to the masara now. We'll come and call you when we are about to leave.'

Thus, my days of misery were going to end. I was going to escape from the goat farm. I couldn't see the future. But it wouldn't hold so much suffering, I was sure. Allah, most merciful, all praises are for you. All glory is yours.

I ran back to the masara. My bag was there on the cot. A bag crumbling from the sun, the rain, the cold, the wind and the sand. A century of dust caked on it. I tried to brush the dust off and open the zip. The top of the bag got ripped off as I pulled at it strongly. A pungent smell came from it. I had not opened the bag for a long time now. There was no need for it. The pickle Sainu had packed from home was still there. An unrecognizable black, dry thing. It was leftover from what I had eaten with khubus in the first days. I hadn't finished it, but kept it safely inside the bag to hang on to Sainu's warmth and smell. When my hopes of meeting Sainu ever again began to dwindle I must have forgotten about the pickle.

I fished out the pair of pants and the shirt I had had stitched before I came to the Gulf. One wouldn't expect silverfish to survive in the desert. But those brand new clothes were completely decomposed and were useless! The corrosiveness of the desert wind was more powerful than that of sea salt. I wondered how much that wind must have corroded me. I didn't have anything to take home. An empty-handed return. I threw the bag away.

The goats were getting restive inside the masara, as if they had sensed my leaving. When I walked into the masara, they gathered around me. If you leave, who is there for us, their eyes seemed to ask me anxiously. I was unlikely to meet these goats ever again in my life. My dear brothers, I am leaving. If I remain here any longer, I will die. I must escape from here. Never from you, but from my own fate. I like each one of you. I would have died long ago had you not been there. It is you, your love, that has helped me survive for so long. Wherever in the world I go, I will remember you as the brothers who were with me through my misery. I will always love you. It is Allah who brought me to my ill fate in this masara. It is He who delivers me now. I will pray to Him to release you too from this fate. Goats, my friends, my brothers, my blood, goodbye.

The goats came to me one by one. Aravu Ravuthar was the first. I stroked his cheeks. I advised him not to break the hands of the unfortunate one who might come instead of me (may no one else suffer this fate ever again), but to work together courteously. He nodded his head. Next Pochakkari Ramani. She wept. I did too. Then, Marymaimuna. I kissed her. She kissed me back. I told her to give her love to the one who came next. She bowed her head sadly. Then Indipokkar, Njandu Raghavan, Parippu Vijayan, Chakki, Ammini, Kausu, Raufat. I bade goodbye to everyone.

I wanted to weep when I reached the masara of the young goats. I felt like the midwife who had to part from the children who were born into her hands. I had been there when most of them were born. I had been their father and mother since. I had fed them. For a second, I thought of Nabeel. My heart ached from the loss. I lifted up Pinki, Ammu, Razia and Thahira and caressed them. They didn't bounce away as they used to whenever I went to catch them. They crawled into my hands and into the warmth of my chest. Children, I know your fate when you grow up. You are to be dragged to the market and to the slaughterhouses. I shall pray to Allah to give you the strength to face that enormous destiny. That's all this poor Najeeb can do. Weeping, I came out of that masara.

I went to the masara of the camels. They were saddened about my departure. The camels were creatures who didn't give me any trouble. They came and went on their own. When they came they needed a little fodder and water. They were content with that. I could read from their expressions that they loved me. I saw love pouring out of their eyes. We wept, as I hugged them and they hugged me. I don't have any human being to say goodbye to. All I have is you. You are the ones who kept me alive all these days. As I am to Allah, forever shall I be indebted to you. I wept some more.

Even while heading towards freedom, it is agonizing to depart from our loved ones. I experienced intense grief in that happy moment of freedom.

Far away, Hakeem's call was heard. I came out of the masara. The goats cried out together. I didn't look back. Had I looked back, maybe I wouldn't have been able to leave that place. Hakeem and Ibrahim Khadiri were waiting for me. We left together. To a new world, to a new life.

Escape
|=======|

Thirty-one

Throughout the night, we ran like mad, as if the sky was on fire. There was no specific route to the masara. The vehicles that came there had made a sandy road. We ran beside it, so as to not lose our way. We didn't know where that path led. Winding through sand dunes that stretched as far as the eyes could reach, that path disappeared into a distant hill slope. Beyond that point, I had only seen the dust raised by vehicles. Anyhow, that path would meet a highway somewhere, we were sure. But we had no idea how long it would take us to get there.

Running wasn't hard at all, as the moon was bright. We felt that both Allah and nature were with us. All through the way, we didn't talk or even glance at one another. We just ran. Despite all that running, a feeling that we had not reached far enough, a panic that someone was after us, constantly followed us. We feared that every sound and whirr of the wind was that of the arbab's vehicle. Therefore, the speed of our running only increased with each second.

After running like that for a long time, we reached a point where that mud trail forked into two different paths. One to the left and one to the right. We faced enormous uncertainty about which road to take to get to the highway. After a lot of discussion, we decided to take the left path. We began to run again.

After running for some more time, a ray of light appeared from far away. When we listened to the sound, we realized that it was a vehicle, moving slowly, swinging and rocking. I felt relief. We had reached the highway. The final means to our deliverance. Suddenly Ibrahim pulled us behind a sand dune. The vehicle was coming in our direction. We could not risk being seen. It could be our arbab. Or some other familiar Arab. Then we would be taken straight to the spot of the arbab's wedding feast. Moving away from the vehicle's path, we hid behind the dune. The vehicle crawled past us. Only after it passed us completely did we recognize that it was a mini-lorry. Its driver was the Pathan who brought hay to our masara. Oh, he knew me. Ibrahim thumped his chest. 'He will save us!' Shouting loudly, all three of us ran after the vehicle. But by the time we reached the road, the vehicle was very far away.

The frustration and sorrow I felt! I even cursed my destiny and the Lord himself. What greater sorrow than watching your luck zoom past you? Angrily, I pulled my hair and beat my chest.

'What is gone is gone. It can never be retrieved. What's the use of lamenting over it? We will find another way,' Ibrahim Khadiri said.

We decided to wait there and try our luck with the next vehicle. The desert sprawled out dead on its back, desolate and empty. I prayed intently, Allah, let any driver, any familiar person, come our way. But no vehicle came in our direction.

Each of our decisions affect our future lives in one way or another. Now when I look back, I see that it would have been better for us to have waited there. But that night we didn't think we could afford to waste any time. We felt that it would be stupid to wait. We had to get away as far as possible, as soon as possible. In the morning, the sun would light up everything; there would be no place for us to hide in the desert. When the arbab reached the masara and realized that we were not there, he would come with his binoculars and the gun. He would spot us in the desert, wherever we were. Then our fate would be that of the scary figure's. We didn't want that to happen to us. We thought since we had decided to escape, we must escape.

Again, we began to run. Now let me tell you something. If you are in the midst of misfortune, whatever you do will be in the order of first-rate stupidity. I say this from experience. If one thinks logically, we should have run in the direction of the vehicle. But, in our perplexed state, we ran the other way. That stupendous mistake is an example of how panic and perplexity put us out of our rational minds. In retrospect I can only console myself with the thought that this was destined to happen in my life and that I merely ran into my destiny.

We ran as fast as we could, keeping ourselves to the side of the road. The arbab had a vehicle and we were on foot. Within five minutes the arbab could reach what we covered in one hour. So we tried to get as far away as we could within one night and find a safe haven to hide.

As we ran we realized something—we were not alone. There were other masaras scattered over the desert. There too, unfortunate men like us were guarding goats. We saw a couple of masaras along the way which proved to be big hazards—because all the arbabs were not out attending weddings. Even a blind arbab would recognize us as absconders. Our appearance gave us away. Therefore, we ran maintaining a certain distance from the path. But there was another problem. As I mentioned earlier, the moon was bright. If we ran through the plains, anyone could spot us from a distance. And no one would mistake our three ugly figures for those of djinns. So, we ran by sand dunes and hills to have as much cover as possible. But that landed us in more trouble.

One of the hillocks we climbed led us straight into a masara. We didn't have time to hide. Someone had spotted us. Besides, Hakeem stepped on someone as he ran. When the man got up and looked around he saw some figures running past him. He began to shout 'Thief! Thief!' He was not alone in that masara. Hearing him, others in the masara woke up and ran after us, trying to catch us. We scampered past them.

Their arbab must have woken up by then. We heard some shouts in Arabic. Suddenly someone pushed me down from behind. I fell on my face. In the next instant I heard a gunshot. Had I not fallen then, a bullet would have pierced my back. 'Don't get up,'

Ibrahim said, lying close to the ground. When they looked, they could not see us anywhere. They seemed astounded. They must have thought that we were indeed djinns. The three of us began to crawl slowly. Our hunters fired aimlessly in the dark for a while before turning back. We crawled and hid behind a sand dune. It was only after ensuring that they had all left that we started running again.

As we ran, I thanked Ibrahim for his kindness and common sense in pushing me down at the nick of time. He was surprised. 'Me? You were not within my reach. Moreover, I wasn't expecting a gunshot at all.'

'Hakeem, was it you?'

'No, not me,' he said.

How did I fall down, I wondered. Apprehensively we looked at each other. Only then did we realize the presence of a fourth among us. Filled with gratitude my eyes began to overflow.

Thirty-two

Only around daybreak did we end our marathon through the desert—hurtling, halting, falling, rising and dashing past hill, sand dune and ditch. At some point in the night the moonlight had disappeared and the desert turned into a cavern of darkness. Still, we kept running for our lives through that wilderness.

Hakeem was the first to stop. 'Enough. I can't. I need some rest.' He fell to the ground panting. We were sure that we had covered a lot of distance and would not be caught soon. In that belief I too sat down with him. Actually, I fell down by him. My feet were aching severely. I was panting like a dog. My throat was so dry that I couldn't utter a word. My heart pounded so heavily it threatened to break my ribcage any moment. My vision was blurred. After sitting for some time, I felt like lying down. Uncaring of the possibility of snakes or centipedes, spreading out my arms, I collapsed. But Ibrahim's face showed no signs of fatigue. He came and sat with us as though he was enjoying the cool breeze after some light work. Before his great strength, we lay there curled up like stray dogs.

At dawn a new sun came calling—of freedom, of new life. I woke up rubbing my eyes as I heard Ibrahim call us. At some point, we had fallen deeply asleep. For a panicky moment, I thought I was in the masara and it was the arbab calling me. But when I opened my eyes, there was no masara in front of me—no goats, no camels, no arbab, no tent. Hakeem was lying nearby, curled up. Suddenly, I became alert. Coming to life, I shook Hakeem. 'Hakeem, do you see, this is where we are. Our days in hell are over. Now we are free forever. Allah, thank you. Lord of all beings, your benevolence is great. Your love is immeasurable.' I wept looking at the sky. I shook Hakeem and called him again. Knocking my hand away, he turned over. He was enjoying the deep sleep of freedom. The freedom to lie down till one had had enough sleep. I left him sleeping. Stretching my back, I looked all around. There were small hills and sand dunes all around. I couldn't see very far. I looked for Ibrahim Khadiri. He was standing on a sand dune, peering into the distance.

'Ibrahim, can you see a road from there?' I called out. He didn't say anything, but motioned me towards him. Anxious about what awaited me, I climbed up the sand dune. Desert! A real desert! An endless stretch of sand as far as the eye could see in the front and the back, on the right and the left. A sea of undulating sand from horizon to horizon! There was nothing to hinder my sight. No tree. No plant. No hill. Nothing at all. Nothing.

It was only then that I got a general idea about the place I had reached. While running we hadn't noticed when our feet lost contact with hard soil and sunk into loose sand. A cold fear slithered into my mind. I looked at the face of Ibrahim Khadiri. Anxiety was writ on his face too. Hakeem alone hadn't been infected by that terror yet. He was still deep asleep.

Ibrahim and I looked at each other. Allah, where have we reached? Where did we come from? Where should we go now? Where is the world we came looking for? East, west, south or north? Which direction will take us to our destination? Who knows! There was only sand all around. Dunes of sand. Had it been another occasion, the picturesque vastness of that sea of sand would have held romantic appeal for me. But at that point, that sea really frightened me.

Not even a canoe or a boat would do, one needed a big ship to cross it. Lord, how can we cross it? Without a drop of water, without a morsel of food? Once the sun is truly up, it will breathe all its heat on us. Can we make it before that? Lord, you are our refuge. May our infinite faith in you save us.

'Ibrahim, do you remember, the whole of yesterday we were running westward. Let's keep going in that direction. It would be impossible to not reach a highway,' I said.

Without replying, he paced up and down anxiously. Finally, after a lot of deliberation, he said, 'The city is in the east. We will walk towards the east.'

We woke Hakeem up. I realized something when he rose and brushed the sand off himself. Hakeem had a terrible stench—the same stench that I had identified when I first reached the masara. I had long stopped noticing that smell. But it came back after I left the masara. In fact, I too had the same stench. But it took me many more days to smell it on myself.

We began to walk. It should have been a time to rejoice as our dreams of freedom had finally materialized. But we were worried. The arbabs must have returned and would be looking for us. The realization that all three of us had escaped together would surely enrage my arbab. Where would he have taken his vehicle to find us? Anyway, arbab, we are not in the direction in which you are searching for us. We have arrived far beyond your reach.

But had we really run far enough to be safe? We had yet to cross this desert and find the highway. Some driver would have to take pity on us and take us to the city. Everything would be over if we are spotted by some Arab. From our looks and our clothes, anyone could tell at a glance that we were running away from a masara. My mind was filled with more anxiety than elation. Still, we kept walking, hope pulsating in us. Sleep had helped us regain our energy, we no longer felt the fatigue that had weighed us down the previous night. The conviction that we were not slaves but free men made us march onwards with gusto.

I had no idea that there was a momentous desert odyssey ahead of us.

Thirty-three

The heat of the desert didn't even touch us. We had withstood its heat and thirst every day. The desert can't easily overpower someone who has been in a masara for many years. It is only those who live in palaces and head out to the desert out of curiosity or for fun who get tired in its heat. We would reach our destination when the desert allowed it. We had Allah with us. It was our faith and confidence that helped us bravely walk through that desert.

We started to enjoy the sights. It was as if we were going for a festival. Hakeem was the liveliest. He wanted to know the what, the why and the how of each and every thing. In a childlike manner, he asked Ibrahim many questions. Ibrahim, who had immense knowledge about the desert, patiently answered him.

We were really fascinated when we reached a forested valley that had been fossilized over time by the constant sand coatings of ceaseless sandstorms. A place beyond our imagination. Several sand mounds were scattered over a large area. Hakeem was very curious and went down into that valley to touch one. Sand began falling off that mound. I wondered how many centuries of sandstorms had resulted in the transformation of the trees and vegetation of the forest. Fearfully, I imagined the desert as a dense forest with the dust storms gradually devouring it.

'We should not stay here for long. It could be a very dangerous place. A sandstorm might come unexpectedly. Then we might never escape,' Ibrahim said.

We had hardly taken ten steps when, suddenly, we saw some movement in front of us. Initially we thought it was water, the alluring illusion of a mirage. Then a hissing sound became audible. Was this the sandstorm Ibrahim had warned us about, we wondered. When we looked carefully, the image ahead danced and swayed, like a garden nodding in the wind. Besides, it was inching ahead. Ibrahim cried out in dread, 'Snakes!' Only then did we see clearly. A battery of snakes swaying their heads and slithering forward. Not one or two. It was probably many hundreds or a thousand, in unison. Again, a sight beyond our imagination. They were marching towards us like a huge army, stirring the dust of the desert. There was a huge snake in the front, like a commander, raising its head. Behind it, many soldiers!

'Hide your head in the sand and don't move. There's nothing else we can do,' Ibrahim said.

Like ostriches we hid our heads in the sand, and lay still. After a while, the hissing approached us. My body was trembling with fear. Ten seconds would suffice for death to come if the fang of one of those creatures even slightly grazed my body. Calling out to Allah very loudly in my mind, I lay still. They moved forward, crawling above us. As each one touched my body, my skin seared as if stroked by a fiery stick. We slowly lifted our heads and looked when we felt sure that they were at a safe distance. All those parts of our bodies that were bare had been blistered as if lashed by whips.

If you are unfamiliar with deserts, you may wonder if this desert was a desert at all. Swarming with living beings it was almost a forest. Snakes, centipedes, lizards, spiders, butterflies, vultures, wolves, rabbits, mongooses and so many other creatures like them. Each with their own paths, their own territories, their own laws—man, his law and his life had no significance here. These creatures didn't value human boundaries. They were the inheritors of the desert. Allah had bequeathed this space to them. They had been created to live here. And I was the trespasser. The blisters on my body were merely their gentle chastening.

We did not have much problem during the day but had to be careful at night. After sunset, those creatures who hid in holes emerged to catch their prey. Those snakes were dreadfully poisonous. There were more than fifty types of snakes. How many snakeskins did we see strewn all along the desert as we walked! Ibrahim would pick one up and tell us about the snake it came from, and also about the number of seconds it would take that snake to kill us with its bite. Even the bite of some desert spiders and centipedes could kill humans.

Do you know that there are tortoises in the desert? Though not as big as sea turtles, they are of a considerable size. They come out when it is not very hot. They live for about a hundred years and almost forty per cent of their body is water. Even camels, whom we call the ships of the desert, have to drink water once in three days. But the desert tortoises have the ability to store water for six months.

The one creature that I wanted to see in the desert, but couldn't, was the ostrich. The sight of it hiding its head in the sand still remains only a dream. Another creature I had heard about was the camel spider—that it gnaws away the belly of the camel running at twenty-five kilometres an hour by clinging to its side and that it was as big as an Arab dining plate and so on. When I actually saw it, I understood that whatever I had heard was an exaggeration. It was Ibrahim who pointed one out to me as we were striding through the desert. Since I had imagined them to be quite large, I wondered if the ones I saw were baby spiders. Ibrahim smiled. What I had heard were fictitious accounts about the poor thing. Everything else, other than that it spent its brave life in the harsh desert, was hyperbole.

The desert wonder I saw was the flying chameleon. While walking in the afternoon sun, a gold tint flashed across my sight and disappeared. The chameleons were like djinns or ghosts. They would vanish in the flash of a second. I wondered if it was an illusion created by my tired and heat-dried eyes. They would appear abruptly from the sand and gaze at us, their eyes flickering from left to right as though they were terrified. Sometimes we could see them flying to some distance. In fact, their zooming made it seem like someone was hurling stones from behind us. Many a time I looked back to see if it was so. Then, another flying figure would emerge from the folds of the sand, to leap and soar. I would have never imagined them to be chameleons.

Then, one day, when we climbed up a sand dune, there they were, playing a game of golden hues. They looked like finches prancing up and down some tree branch. About a hundred of them were frolicking in that sand lake. I wanted to catch one and find out if it had wings or if it flew using only its legs. But they flew and dived into the sand so quickly that, forget catching, I could barely see one closely. 'These chameleons never drink water,' Ibrahim Khadiri said. If you can live a whole life without drinking water, chameleons, oh golden chameleons who made this phase of my arduous journey so happy, please gift me a trace of that ability so that I can complete this journey.

Around noon the air became opaque with dust and we felt sleepy. We couldn't see past ten feet. That made our walk even more difficult. It felt as though it was fire that lit up the day and not sunshine. As the heat increased, our bodies wilted. The exuberance that had pumped us up at the beginning of the day had slowly evaporated. But Ibrahim kept encouraging us. 'Another mile, and we might reach the highway!' After all it is only hope that makes a man go forward. We walked. But before our eyes it was only the desert that rolled out endlessly. Sand, sand and more sand.

The afternoon passed too and it was evening. We still didn't find the only thing that we were looking for. The sun that crawled above us to the west deserted us in the wilderness and rode out alone into the horizon. After a day spent without a drop of water to moisten the tongue, the night approached. Gasping and exhausted, we sat on the sand. I broke down. The agony of not reaching anywhere even after a whole day of walking left me in tears. Hakeem joined me in my tears.

In the first days when I reached this country I had often longed to live in a beautiful desert, a desert where sand stretched out like sea. But when I finally came upon a beautiful desert it terrified me. We have heard many stories of those who had to cross the desert. We have read that they were thrilled by their adventures. But all of them were assisted in their voyage by strong camels. To help them, they had the Bedouins, who knew the desert like the lines on their palms. Their bags were filled with food and they had leather canteens full of water. Those who had tried to cross this desert on their own, without food and water, must have fainted in the sand and died, not living to tell their tales. Allah, are we to become like them? We didn't come to the desert looking for fun. Nor out of curiosity. We came to live. To be alive. To meet once again the beautiful faces of those who love us. To wipe the tears they shed for us from their cheeks. We have reached this spot in our effort to do so. Allah, only you, only your strength, only your way, only your safety can protect us. Please Allah, don't kill us by roasting us in this desert.

Thirty-four

The next day Ibrahim Khadiri woke us up long before dawn, 'Let's walk before it gets hot.'

My swollen legs were heavy as an elephant's as I got up. Ignoring the pain, we dragged our feet through the loose sand. After we walked a short distance, the sun appeared on the eastern arch. We knew that it would set the sand ablaze.

The sky seemed like an upturned grey-blue basket covering us from above. One side of it began at some corner of the desert. It gradually went up to reach its high point above my head and then slowly came down to its rim in another corner. We were like chickens trapped inside that basket. Somehow, we had to lift it and get outside. But to do that we had to at least reach its rim. A rim that, despite all the walking, we had so far failed to reach. A sense of endlessness engulfed us. Nothing registered in my view but the sheer blue of the sky and the blazing sun.

'Don't panic,' Ibrahim consoled us. 'The horizon is merely two and a half miles from us. And perhaps just beyond that is the path we are looking for. Don't get dejected, walk with hope. Once we get tired, we will fall down under this sun for the rest of the day. So walk as well as you can, even if it is a struggle. We have to find a secure place as soon as possible.'

After walking for a while, we came across the signs of a river that had drained into the desert long ago. I was amazed. In that burning heat it was difficult to imagine that a river once ran through these sands. But its lines were still distinct. I visualized how men in the past stood on its shore and drowned while trying to cross it. At the same shore where they died swallowing water, I suffered as my parched throat cried for a drop of water. How far is that moment in the past from my situation? What might have happened in the interim? I imagined the river slowly drying up and the living beings in it gradually perishing. I could hear the trees and shrubs on its banks lament for water. Time, how strange is your face!

By then we had spent two nights and a day and a half without a drop of water on our tongues. We could barely keep our eyes open. We walked in a state of half sleep. When we crossed all boundaries of tolerance of our condition, Hakeem began to moan for water. The problem is we are used to excessive use of water. Man can easily survive without food or water for up to fourteen days. 'Try to walk thinking about Allah,' Ibrahim admonished him.

But Hakeem kept on asking for water. All along the way. After walking for some more time, he grabbed my hand. 'No, ikka. I can't. You carry on. Let me lie down here.'

I scolded him, 'Hakeem, don't give up. Don't fall down. Walk.' Then I chanted to him, 'Allahu Akbar. Allahu Akbar.' He repeated along with me, 'Allahu Akbar.' It was as if that chant and its resonance brought us a new strength. With that energy we walked for a while longer. Then slowly our walk began to lose its vigour and vitality. Our weary legs would not take us any further. We were so exhausted that numbness and pain overwhelmed us. The skin of our feet had become sore from the heat of the sand. Hakeem's feet were already swollen. But drawing on his remaining strength he dragged his legs and tried to go on. Within the next few seconds, we realized to our horror that it was not possible any more.

Worn out, Hakeem fell to the ground. As if I had been waiting for him to fall, I also lay down near him.

Ibrahim scolded us, 'Get up. This rest will only make you tired. It will not refresh you. This sun will drain the last drop of water from your body. Don't fry your body like this in the sand, just go on for a bit longer. The sand will get cool. The desert cools fast. Then you can rest. Haven't we endured this long enough? Hold on for just a bit longer.'

'Off you go, dog!' Hakeem cried in anguish. 'Have you got us out to be killed? Is this what you had promised us? We were better off in the masara. Even the arbab's torture was not as bad as this. I can't! I am tired. Let me die if I have to. You can save yourself if you want.'

I saw Ibrahim Khadiri's eyes getting wet for the first time during that journey. Helplessly, he raised his hands to the heavens. Then he knelt down and prayed.

The desert was boiling. I felt as if I was lying in Allah's frying pan. Still, that rest after the long trek brought me relief. Initially I found the heat unbearable. But after lying like that for some time, I got used to it. By then, the sun, the desert and I were equally hot. What remained distinct was the insatiable thirst. But there was no way to quench it. Even the last drop of spittle in my mouth had dried long ago. I beat my breast and cursed my foolishness for not taking a little water in a bottle or some vessel before we ran away. We had left at a moment when all sense had deserted us. Now we had to face the consequences. What else to do?

We realized that what Ibrahim had said was true. The longer we rested, the more tired our bodies became and the more stubbornly they refused to revive. Darkness entered my eyes. I became dizzy. I vomited twice. After a while, Hakeem also vomited. Ibrahim removed his clothes and tried to make some shade for us with them. But that too was inadequate. He tried to raise us up and make us sit. But we just flopped down. I slipped into a deep sleep. Hakeem and I lay there like two stray dead bodies. If he wanted, Ibrahim could have deserted us and found a route to escape. But he kept watch over us till we opened our eyes when it was finally night.

My throat was aflame when I woke up. But where was the water to soothe it? Allah, how much water have I wasted back home! Now I am begging for a drop of it. I realize the greatness of my homeland. Is this, Allah, the punishment for that waste? Forgive me!

Water. I realized how precious it is.

Thirty-five

Writers in every language and religion have seen the desert as a space for enlightenment and spiritual revival. There are writings that suggest life in the desert can create an explosion of knowledge in the brain. But the desert did not revive me in any way. I lived in the desert for more than three years. Then I tried crossing it. All through, the desert gave me nothing but grief and frustration. Maybe the desert gave spiritual knowledge to those who came seeking it. I didn't set out to look for anything, so I got trapped. It must have decided that it had nothing to offer me.

With no idea of where we were going, we wandered in the desert for another two days. We didn't get anywhere. Nobody saved us. By then we were absolutely tired. The blisters on our feet from walking on the hot sand burst. The swelling had gradually spread to our knees. Unbearable burning. Pain. It must have been about afternoon that day when Hakeem, who had been walking quietly, suddenly rushed forward, shouting 'Water! Water! Allah, water!'

I stared fearfully in the direction in which he was running. I guessed, even with my little experience of travelling in the desert, that it was a mirage. I called him back. But, without heeding my cries, Hakeem ran forward shouting like a madman. Ibrahim and I ran after him and caught him. By then he was frothing at the mouth. Blood was dripping from his nose. I wiped his face with my clothes and we forced him to sit down. He told me he was feeling dizzy. After some time he began to make strange gestures. Suddenly he sprang up like a person who had contracted rabies and ran away.

We ran after him. After running for a while, he fell down exhausted. Then he began to cry very loudly. He pushed us away when we went to catch him and began to eat hot sand. Although Ibrahim and I tried to stop him, he shrugged us off with demonic strength and kept eating sand. Then, he started vomiting. There was nothing Ibrahim or I could do. We were helpless. After vomiting for some time, Hakeem began to spit blood. He writhed in the sand like a beaten snake. His eyes bulged out. More blood began to ooze from his nostrils and mouth along with froth and foam.

'Ibrahim, do something! My Hakeem will die now,' I cried. 'Allah, my Lord, Lord of all the worlds, Let nothing happen . . . Let nothing happen to my Hakeem! Please protect him,' I prayed beating my breast.

I looked at the heavens. The flaming sun met my eyes.

I went to Ibrahim again, crying, 'Do something Ibrahim . . .' He sat unmoving and in my anguish I hit him and kicked him and spat on him.

'We can't do anything but leave Hakeem to Allah's care,' Ibrahim cried. I had never seen Ibrahim look so helpless.

I was shattered. I sank down, closing my eyes. I couldn't watch Hakeem's convulsions. His grunts and shudders lasted for a little while. Slowly, I opened my eyes and glanced at him. He was lying there staring at me. He was trying to say something. I ran to him. 'Dear Hakeem, don't worry!' I took him into my lap. His eyes moved once. Then slowly they became still. A pall of darkness spread over my brain. A deathly fatigue overcame my body. I blacked out.

When I opened my eyes, I was hanging from Ibrahim Khadiri's shoulder like a dead body. The desert was blowing a furious dust storm. Even taking a step forward was difficult. Still, Ibrahim was carrying me on his shoulders and running fast. I couldn't understand why he was running like that. But I was so exhausted that I couldn't get down.

I looked around me as I hung on. There was some movement behind the sand dune. Wondering what it was, I looked carefully. The movement wasn't behind the sand dune, it was the sand dune that was moving. Like a wave comes from the far corner of the sea, a sand wave was moving in from the desert. And behind that came other huge waves. I felt that we were not standing in a desert, but on a beach. The topography was constantly changing before my eyes. The sand dunes would rise up and fall down and vanish into thin air.

'Shut your eyes tightly,' Ibrahim screamed. He put me down and hugged me close. 'Don't move!' We stood there embracing each other. Within a few moments, the fringe of a wave came and touched us. I could feel the hot sand burning my face, body and hands. I don't know how long we had to remain like that in that cave of sand. When I was sure the wind had subsided, I slowly opened my eyes and looked. Embracing me was a sand figure! There was only dust in the air. I couldn't see anything ahead. Sand everywhere. We were almost waist deep in sand. More than that, what amazed me was the fact that the sand mountain in front of me had moved ahead. As if a map had been redrawn in front of us. A mountain like that one have buried my Hakeem forever.

Thirty-six

Somehow Ibrahim dragged himself out of the sand dune and he pulled me out too. He was about to put me on his shoulder and walk when I wriggled out of his grasp. 'Ibrahim, abandon me here and save yourself. I don't want to go anywhere without Hakeem. I don't want to escape. We came together. I can't go home without him. I can't face his ummah's questions or meet his sister's eyes. Leave me here. I want to go with him. I want to go with him!'

I tried to rush towards the sand mountain that had buried Hakeem's body. But Ibrahim grabbed me and forced me on to his shoulder, 'Allah didn't send me to that masara to abandon you like this. I couldn't save Hakeem, but I will permit you to die only after I die.'

I didn't have the strength to resist him. I hung on his shoulder like a wilted plant. I sobbed like a small child. Carrying me, he walked through that sand forest. Thirst, fear and hunger clung to us. I could feel my own heart beat. As moments passed it grew fainter. Even my breath became faint. My tongue felt heavy, as though I could never again move it. The world grew dark and moved around me. Like steam, heat came out of my skull. I began to lose control of my senses. I realized that I was becoming like Hakeem in his final moments. I don't have much time left in this world. It was time to say goodbye. I tried to remember all those who loved me and those whom I loved. Not many human faces came to my mind. Ummah, Sainu, Hakeem . . . But the goats in my masara filled my mind's eye one after another. Nabeel, Aravu Ravuthar, Pochakkari Ramani, Marymaimuna, Indi Pokkar, Njandu Raghavan, Parippu Vijayan, Chakki, Ammini, Kausu, Raufat. Maybe that was because those goats had loved me more than humans did. All of them bade me goodbye.

Evening came. Night came. Again we lay on the sand. A whole night passed during which we did not utter a word to each other. I didn't think I had the strength to live through that night. But I survived. I was alive the next morning.

Thirty-seven

The wind had subsided and the morning was unusually serene. We slowly got up, neither of us uttered a word. Hopes and expectations had come to an end. We only wanted to reach some place. I did not even want to reach any place, I just wanted to die as soon as possible. I couldn't withstand the thirst and the heat any longer. Allah, save us, as you saved Hakeem from this hell.

My feet did not fall firmly on the ground as we walked through the sand. I was walking like a half-dead person. Ibrahim offered to carry me on his shoulders many times. I didn't let him. I knew that I would die that day. Only that much of life was left in my body. I decided to walk hoping I would die more quickly if I walked.

After walking for some time, we spotted the footprints of some creatures on the sand. Light signs of their furtive excursions. Ibrahim followed them and saw where they led. They stretched far and ended in the wild. Confirming that it was the desert's heartland, he led me in the other direction. We might have walked till around noon when all of a sudden we spotted a big lizard on the sand.

'Lizard!' crying loudly, Ibrahim ran after it. I didn't understand his excitement. I was already swaying in half-sleep. Hoping to fall any time . . .

'Najeeb, did you see that? It was a lizard!' Ibrahim cried joyfully.

'So?' I frowned.

'Do you know what a lizard in the desert means? It means that there's water somewhere near,' he said gleefully.

'Really?' Suddenly, I came awake with hope.

He nodded. 'Now we have to be extremely careful with every step. We shouldn't go back into the desert. This is our last chance,' Ibrahim warned.

Therefore, we walked very carefully. With each step, we looked for more lizards. We moved in the direction towards which they had fled. We had reached the top of a sand dune when I saw it clearly. Green tops at a distance! Date palms. Small shrubs. There had to be water nearby! After that I didn't know whether I was running or flying. Forgetting all fatigue I rushed there.

Although my legs were as heavy as an elephant's, I ran, dragging them along. Although my legs were cut and were bleeding, I ran over stones ignoring them. Ibrahim Khadiri was behind me. Even though I had walked longing for death, the desire to live was deep within me. Maybe it was that craving that helped me hold on to life till the very end.

Since I was sure about the presence of water I ran madly through the thick shrubs. There was the buzz of a thousand bees in my head. A thousand white circles soared in front of my eyes. I could relate to Hakeem's mad gestures in his last moments. I had become mad with thirst. I moved here and there, running in all directions. But Ibrahim looked for water in a calm, systematic manner. He looked for spots with more greenery. Places where the sand was damper. Finally he found a small pool among the shrubs. He raised his hands to the heavens and cried aloud, 'Allahu Akbar! Water! Water! Allahu Akbar!'

My head was ablaze when that sound fell on my ears. I ran towards him like a madman. When I saw it, my eyes opened wide with wonder. A small pool amid the shrubs. So much water! Crazy with thirst, I dashed towards it. Suddenly Ibrahim pulled me away. 'Don't drink!' he shouted. My eyes blazed. My blood boiled. Gathering all my strength, I hit him on his neck. He staggered at that unexpected assault.

Again I moved towards the water. Then Ibrahim caught my legs and dragged me to a distance and laid me down. 'Let me off, dog. I am thirsty! I must drink water,' I screamed.

But he wouldn't let me go. I hit my chest and cried. 'My Lord, why do you make it so difficult for me to get what I long for? Strike this villain down with lightning. I walked with him all these days. He killed Hakeem. Now his plan is to kill me. That crook will finish all the water in the pool. I won't even get to moisten my tongue. I must drink some water before I die. I must know its taste,' I struggled and screamed.

Since Ibrahim had taken me so far away from the pool I had no strength to get up and go towards it. He went to the pool. I closed my eyes unable to bear the sight of him finishing up all that water.

All of a sudden, I felt a dampness on my lips. I opened my eyes. Ibrahim was sitting near me. He had a wet piece of cloth in his hand. He was moistening my lips with that. Greedily, I opened my mouth. As a drop of water from it fell on my tongue, I sprang up as if burned with acid. He again dabbed my mouth with that cloth. Drop by burning drop of water oozed on to my tongue.

Again, Ibrahim went and wet the cloth. Water forced its way through my tongue into my throat. That moistness reached my stomach burning all the sore spots. It was only after my mouth was moistened fully that the burning sensation slowly ebbed and a thirst began to grow in me. Ibrahim walked me to that spring. Scooping water in his palms, he slowly poured it into my mouth. I drank till I was fully satiated. I felt, with pleasure, the wetness spreading to each cell of my body. Finally, after I drank enough, I fell down on the ground exhausted. It was only then that Ibrahim Khadiri took the wet cloth to his own parched tongue for the first time.

I sobbed heavily recalling my pettiness.

Thirty-eight

We stayed at that oasis for the next three days. We drank enough water and ate dates from the palm trees. We slept enough and washed off the fatigue of all those days from our bodies. But the pain, swollen legs and burnt soles remained. Every morning Ibrahim went out to scout the area and returned in the evening. His goal was to locate human presence, so that we could find out more . . . Was there any way for us to get out? Where were we? And so on.

On the very first day, Ibrahim rejected my offer to go with him. 'In the desert, you are like a fast-withering flower. The next step in your journey will begin only after we find a proper route.' I was scared that he would lose his way during his wanderings and not be able to come back for me. I valued his companionship and did not want to be alone on this earth. Worry welled up in me when he was late to return. I couldn't imagine being lonely. I would be at ease only after I caught sight of him on some distant sand dune.

Once Ibrahim Khadiri left for the day, I would walk around the entire oasis. Usually, the greenery of an oasis spreads over many acres. Arabs and travellers visit the place. This was nothing like that. It could have been the world's smallest oasis, it was so tiny. It had a pool, some date palms, some unknown cacti, some small plants. Surrounding this little green patch was an endless stretch of sand. A tiny oasis. God's own Garden of Eden. I often wondered if God had created the oasis only for us.

On the afternoon of the third day, Ibrahim returned happy. It meant that he had seen something that pleased him. Dragging myself, I approached him. 'What, Ibrahim, any signs of a road?'

'We're not very far away from life, Najeeb,' he said. 'Today, I discovered three stones. Three stones used by humans. Some people had come that way. Lit a fire in a hearth made with stones to cook food. It is a good sign.'

The next morning, we walked in that direction. It was pointless to stay in the oasis for much longer. So we left the safety of water to go where Allah would take us. I also saw the stones Ibrahim was excited about. That open area did not have loose sand. As we went around inspecting it, a path slowly became visible. A path made by regular vehicle traffic. More evidence of human presence. It could have been a spot city dwellers frequented for fun. If that was the case, this path would surely lead us to a safe destination! Again our hope that we would be saved began to swell. With that hope we hurriedly followed the path. At each turn, behind every hill, we expected human presence. But that path took us through barren and uninhabited land. Then, we saw it. A long mark, like the lines on the squirrel's back, running through the middle of a sand dune! My ravenous eyes spotted it from far away. Hurriedly I ran towards it.

My suspicion turned out to be correct. It was the mark of wheels. My Lord, *Rabb al alameen*, this mark could signify so many things. That some human being had been here! That there is human presence nearby. That there is a road somewhere nearby. That there is a human settlement somewhere nearby. A little lamp of hope was lit in that great world of darkness.

We decided to follow that track. We firmly believed it would lead us to a secure place. The wheel marks were not of a vehicle belonging to any human being. It was the mark made by the wheels of Allah's vehicle. A pointer to escape. Allah, thank you. A thousand thanks. A billion thanks.

Still we were apprehensive. A breath of wind would have been enough to end all that hope. If the wind turned direction, that wheel mark would dissolve into nothing. But that day, Allah was with us. He did not permit the wind to even stir. Forgetting all our discomfort, we started to run. I forgot the ache in my legs, the twitches, the swelling, the pain, the burning, the cuts, everything. We reached the path before the wind blew it away. Twisting and turning, it went on as we ran alongside. Our dreams also came alive.

I am not sure how long we ran following the flicker of hope. It was dusk when we were sure that we had almost reached our destination. But, in an unfortunate turn of events, the wind which had been dead throughout the day, suddenly sprang up and vigorously carried away the wheel trail on its wings.

We stood shocked. When the storm subsided, only endless emptiness stretched wide open before us. Desperately, I broke into a cry. I looked towards the heavens. 'Enough, Lord, enough. Please don't play games with me any more, Lord. I can't stand being mocked by you any longer.' Ignoring Ibrahim Khadiri's entreaties to go on, I lay over the sand waves, like the remains of a shipwreck. One more evening was washed away in tears.

Thirty-nine

Dawn had not yet broken. I was jolted out of sleep by an unfamiliar sound. It must have been a dream. I closed my eyes. Again that sound. I woke up. The desert, discarding all its fury, was sleeping serenely. One could clearly hear even distant sounds. Again that sound. I listened, paying close attention. When fully loaded vehicles pass through the highway, their tyres make a peculiar sound. How many times had I heard it in the silent hours of the night back at the masara. Surely, this too is the sound of a vehicle moving at some distance, somewhere. I could hear the traffic intermittently.

Before me was a reasonably big hill. There must be a highway on the other side of this hill, unless my senses had completely failed me and this noise was the hallucination of my tired mind. Vehicles passed through that highway! I scrambled up from my sleep. 'Ibrahim!' I screamed. 'We have reached. We have reached.' My mind was fluttering with joy. I ran to where Ibrahim was sleeping. But he wasn't there. I looked all around. Ibrahim wasn't there anywhere.

'Ibrahim! Ibrahim!' I shouted, moving around the place. There was no reply from anywhere. Where had he gone? He had gone to sleep along with me. 'Ibrahim! Ibrahim!' I shouted again and again, searching for him. All those shouts blended into the desert's infinity without any answer.

The first light broke in the desert's eastern corner. The pall of darkness disappeared. Right in front of me, sand and hill came into view. Assisted by the light, I looked around for a long time. Ibrahim Khadiri was nowhere. Climbing up a sand dune, I looked all around. There was no sign of him. It was only after a lot of searching that I accepted the truth. My guide and my saviour Ibrahim Khadiri had disappeared from my life forever. Without leaving a trail.

I felt lonely and sad, as if I was the last man on earth. I cried sitting on the sand. Ibrahim, you left me alone like this, on the way to where? Weren't we together all these days? All through the misery and the sorrow. And here we are, about to reach the road to safety. At most an hour's walk to the highway. But where are you? Where did you disappear last night? You could have told me. You could have said a goodbye, at least.

It was only after the day grew hot that I got up from there and walked. I found that walk a hundred times more difficult than all my days of walking with Ibrahim. I felt like I was moving backwards. How much that solitude hurt me! Finally, by about evening I reached the road. It was not a highway on which a lot of vehicles passed. A vehicle came along once in a while. They were mostly trailers carrying heavy loads. Infrequently, some cars screamed past. Worn out, I extended my hand at every vehicle. But all the vehicles ignored me and went on their way, leaving me very frustrated. As each vehicle moved away, I kept hoping that the next one would surely stop for me and take me along. But luck was not with me. No driver showed any sympathy. Rather, Allah didn't direct any driver to do so. Thus, I passed one more night orphaned by Allah.

Forty

Day broke. The flow of vehicles, which had almost ceased in the last quarter of the night, started again. Most of them were vehicles carrying heavy loads. Going down to the middle of the road, I waved my hand at each vehicle. That day too every vehicle ignored me and drove past me. I wasn't surprised. Seeing the shape that I was in after three years in a masara, people would not have wanted to take me along. And after many days of wandering in the desert, I had completely ceased to resemble a human being.

My hunger and thirst kept growing. It had already been three days since we set off from the oasis. I just couldn't imagine losing my life after coming this close to freedom. I hated myself as Allah wouldn't look at me. What sin had I committed to deserve this? I asked, beating my chest. Allah, you made me lose both my friends in the desert. The desert dried Hakeem to death and made Ibrahim vanish. You have brought me till here. For what? For what? It remains unanswered in my mind.

The afternoon blaze soon set in. More vehicles kept moving past me. I saw a very expensive car zooming in from afar. I knew there was no use waving at it. Why would the driver let me get into such a car when even trailer drivers sneered at me! Still something inside me urged me to wave at the car as it drew near. Naturally, it didn't stop and went past me. But, at a short distance past me, it screeched to a halt. I was surprised. Did it stop because I signalled? After wondering for a second if the car had actually stopped for me, I ran towards it. Inside it was a handsome, richly dressed Arab. Lowering the car window, he asked me something. I didn't know what to answer. Revered Arab, how many vehicles have gone past me since yesterday. Nobody stopped for me. You didn't ask what do you want, why are you staying here, how did you land here. You felt like applying your feet on the brake for me. Enough. That is sufficient for me. Unconsciously, my eyes overflowed.

The Arab didn't ask me anything after that. He opened the back door of his vehicle for me. He beckoned me to sit inside. Then he drove down the road with me.

I hesitated to sit straight on the spotless seat of that splendid vehicle. Still, I sat. Some time after I got in, he switched off the air conditioner and lowered the windows. He covered his nose. I knew it was because of my stench. Had he wanted, he could have thrown me out of the car. But he didn't show any annoyance. I asked that great man for some water. He gave me a bottle of water. I emptied it at one go. He asked me if I wanted another bottle. I nodded my head. He gave me another one. I drank that too. Still my thirst was not quenched. But politeness restrained me from asking for more.

Slowly I reclined on the seat. I was so tired I soon fell asleep. So, I don't know how long I travelled. I only woke up when the vehicle stopped in a city area. It was almost evening by then. I looked all around perplexed. Very huge buildings. Many people and a lot of commotion. Heavy traffic. After travelling for some more distance, the Arab parked the car by the side of the road and looked back at me. I understood that was my signal to get down. How could I express my gratitude to that great man who tolerated me for so long? In return for his goodwill, I could only give him a teardrop. He didn't ask anything. He didn't say a word.

I got out of the vehicle and shut the door. Leaving me alone in the middle of the city, the Arab sped away.

I wept. I had realized that Allah occasionally travels even in a luxury car.

Forty-one

Eyes wide open, I stood in that area for some time. I could see those who went past me stare at me like I was a strange creature. I walked slowly, keeping to the side of the road. It was a market alongside a long, winding road. All around were heaps of vegetables and fruits. Their soft odour hung in the air. Crowds of Arabs flowed like a river. Women, with only their eyes showing, moved around in black robes. There were many Indian vendors. The sound of commerce. And among them all, I stood out looking like a primitive man. Everyone stared at me and tried to skirt around me to avoid touching me. I didn't feel hurt. In fact, even I could smell my stink.

I was very hungry. But I didn't have any money to buy food. During my life in the Gulf, that was the first occasion when I felt the need for money. Had I been in the masara, I could have eaten the arbab's khubus at least. I didn't need money for that. I could have eaten the wheat meant for the goats. Money wasn't required for that either. But one had to pay money to eat anything in the city. Who would give me food without money in exchange? I tried to enter one or two shops. I even begged for food. But their owners drove me away as if I were a despicable stray dog.

With hope springing anew in my heart, I walked through that market. I felt dizzy after walking for some time. I must have walked a little further when I spotted a board with 'Malabar Restaurant' written on it. Such relief! An assurance that someone who could understand my language was in there. Someone who could understand what I said. I steeled myself and walked towards it.

I have no recollection of what happened after I reached the place. Later I heard that I fainted on the steps.

Refuge

Forty-two

In every Arab city, there is a loving, shelter-giving banyan tree.

It was in front of Kunjikka's hotel, a refuge for Malayalis in Batha market, that I had fainted. Note the loving ways of Allah. I, who was a stranger to that market, could have strayed anywhere and could have fainted elsewhere. Nobody would have cared for me. But Allah had decided that I was to reach Kunjikka. So I walked that way, reached the doorsteps of the Malabar Restaurant and fell down. He had trusted Kunjikka's heart to take care of the rest.

On the third day after reaching the city, when I opened my eyes, I found myself in Kunjikka's room. When I regained consciousness there was a heavy ache in my hands and legs. There was a needle in my arm and I had been on a drip. I wondered if I was in a hospital. Still, seeing Malayalis around me, I wept. Taking my hand in his, Kunjikka consoled me. I had become a topic of conversation among the Malayalis of Batha. When they heard I had regained consciousness, many of them rushed into the room. They brought me apples, oranges, grapes and bananas as gifts. Everyone wanted to know my story. How did I end up in that state? How did I land there? Their curiosity was written on their faces. But nobody asked me anything. It was only after another two days, after a doctor came, examined me and removed the drip, that Kunjikka gently asked me for my story.

'I need a mirror,' I said.

'Why a mirror?' Kunjikka, who was sitting beside me, asked.

'I just want to see myself.'

The others present stared at one another.

I just wanted to see myself as everyone saw me, the man everyone thought was pitiable.

One of them brought me a small mirror. I looked at myself. I stared at it for a long time. I couldn't recognize myself at all. The person I saw there was a stranger. His hair was cut short, his beard shaved off. The man in the mirror was not the one who had set off from the homeland. I was someone else altogether. A dark, frail, skinny figure with protruding teeth. Had I been told on any other occasion that the person I saw in the mirror was me, I would not have believed it.

Kunjikka explained to me how he and his workers held me as I fainted and brought me into his restaurant to give me food and water; how I was taken to his room; how, with tender care, he bathed me on that day, the next and the day after; how a barber was brought in to cut my hair and shave my beard; how a doctor was brought in to examine and treat me. But my unconscious mind had not registered any of these events.

I had nothing to give them except my tears. I didn't even have any love to give in return. I had only one regret, that they didn't take my photo before cutting my hair and beard. I never got to see the primitive shape I had been in. Today, I don't have any evidence to produce before you as proof of that life. Only my experience and memories. Even the passport that testified my arrival in that country was in the custody of the arbab . . .

'What date is it today?' I asked those who were gathered there.

'It's the thirteenth.'

'Which month?'

They frowned. 'August.'

'Which year?'

They became anxious. 'Nineteen ninety-five.'

'Lord! Rabb al alameen . . .' I placed my hands on my chest. Then I calculated the time that had elapsed.

'Three years, four months, nine days.'

Those who heard me were dumbstruck.

Then, after two more days, when I was able to walk a little, Kunjikka took me from that room to the next one. There was a telephone in that room. Kunjikka made me sit before it.

'Don't you want to call home? Don't you want to hear the sound of your ummah and your wife?'

I cried. I didn't have a telephone at home. I told him the telephone number of the Moplah neighbour. I still wonder how I had remembered that number, which I had not used for such a long time. It was from Bombay that I had called that number the last time.

Kunjikka spent a very long time in front of the telephone. The connection wasn't getting through.

Finally the phone rang at the other end. He gave me the receiver. I had to try hard to make my neighbour recognize me. When he finally did, there was a brief silence. Then he asked, 'Where have you been so long, Najeeb?'

I didn't have any answer. I could imagine the many stories that might have spread about me back home.

'Call after quarter of an hour. I will fetch your wife,' he said.

Those fifteen minutes were longer than the three years I had spent in the masara. Kunjikka finally dialled the number again.

This time, it was easy. Kunjikka gave me the receiver. I only said hello. I heard the loud wailing of my Sainu at the other end. Then for a long time, both of us could only cry. She didn't ask anything. Where have you been? Why haven't you called till now? Sitting there, she must have read my mind.

After crying for some time, she said, 'Our son Nabeel has started going to kindergarten this year. Don't you want to see him? When is ikka coming home? Ikka, our ummah is no more. Last year. She died heartbroken, not hearing a word about you . . .'

I didn't have the strength to hear anything more. I put the receiver down. My mind throbbed with pain. Covering my face, I wept. Kunjikka consoled me.

'Haven't you suffered so much, Najeeb? All that that was given to you was given by Allah. We don't have any right to question His will.'

Feeding on Kunjikka's generosity, I stayed with him for a period of three months. There, in the shelter he provided, my wounds healed. The swelling on my legs reduced. I regained my health. And at different times, I recounted my story to Kunjikka and friends. Many of them refused to believe my story. Only a few believed me. Even those who believed me, found the disappearance of Ibrahim Khadiri inexplicable. Their doubts were justified. I don't have any proper explanation to offer.

Ibrahim Khadiri. My saviour. My liberator in the desert. My Prophet Moses. Where might he have disappeared after bringing me to the gate of safety? Like you, I don't know.

It was while I was getting better that Hameed sought refuge in Kunjikka's room. He had been working as a labourer in an Arab's farm. He had to work hard till night and undergo much abuse for too little compensation. He absconded when it became intolerable. Having him for company was a relief. Otherwise I felt dreadfully lonely in the apartment once Kunjikka and his friends left to work in the restaurant. His presence made my life pleasant.

Then, after several days of planning, and following the advice and directions of many, we decided to give ourselves up to the police without delay and somehow land in prison.

Forty-three

Looking intently at each face, the arbab walked past the line. With his every step, my heart pounded loudly. I couldn't imagine a return to the masara. Allah, again? I just can't. Show me some mercy. My heart burnt and wept. But I didn't wail like Hameed. I stood there audaciously. That wait seemed to last forever. Finally, the arbab came and stood before me. He stared at me. I could see the sand dunes moving in waves in his eyes. Their fierceness frightened me. But I didn't budge. I stood there waiting for the moment when I would be dragged out of the line. After standing there for a long time, the arbab tapped me on my shoulder once. Then, as if he didn't recognize me, he moved on to the next one. I don't know what made the arbab who had come to catch me change his heart. It was a miracle, a great miracle. How else can I explain it? But the arbab left after throwing in a shovel of burning coals of doubt in my mind.

After the parade was over, I told a friendly policeman that my arbab had been present among the Arabs who had come that day and it was only by the grace of Allah that he left without taking me along. The policeman replied that the arbab had gone back saying, 'It's just that he is not under my visa, otherwise I would have dragged him back to the masara!' I was shocked. Either the arbab had lied to mask the pity he had shown his prey or he had revealed a horrible truth. Wasn't he my sponsor then? Had he illegally held me captive? On that day at the airport, had he kidnapped me? Was I brought on someone else's visa? Then Allah . . . did you make me suffer someone else's fate?

Karuvatta's brother-in-law later swore that he had not arranged for a shepherd's visa for me. It was the visa of a helper in a construction company. Lord only knew who spoke the truth. I am not going to lose my sleep thinking about it. It was my destiny to walk into that life. I overcame it. I am not going to think any deeper about it. If I did, I would surely become crazy.

Three more weeks passed. I spent all those days fearing the arbab would come back with forged documents. But he didn't. He must have got someone else. May Allah's mercy be with that hapless one.

As usual, the embassy officials came the day after an Arab parade. We all stood in line. They called out the names one after another. I was standing there as usual without any hope. Suddenly I thought I heard my name. I hesitated for a second. Was it my name they had called? Or was it my imagination? But they called it out again. 'Najeeb Muhammad.' This time I heard it clearly. My name, indeed! I moved forward with a racing heart. Hearing my name, all those who were there with me shed tears of joy. Among them, I had the most seniority in prison.

That day eighty of us got a 'free out pass' to India. It was part of a government project to deport unauthorized residents to the countries of their origin. So Kunjikka didn't have to raise any money for my ticket. I am sure he would have done so had it been necessary. Kunjikka was that kind of person.

As the embassy people prepared the release papers, I said goodbye to all those who were with me. I consoled everyone. I met the policemen and bade them goodbye.

In the warden's office, we were made to sign some papers. Then we were handcuffed. Later, we were made to stand in a line in a corner. Then, by noon, a bus came. That bus went straight to the airport. We were led inside through a special door. I couldn't even ring up Kunjikka to tell him I was free. He must have learned about it from someone. I still regret that I had to leave before I could say a good word to him. If you happen to read this from some corner of the earth, I hope that you will forgive me for the lapse.

Our return flight was at night. The embassy officials distributed the boarding passes. Together, we were made to walk towards the plane. I could not help thinking how the sight was so similar to herding a flock of goats back into a masara! I was one of the goats. Mine was a goat's life.

Author's note

One day, my friend Sunil told me a story about a person called Najeeb. I thought it to be one of the typical sob-stories from the Gulf. I didn't take it seriously. But Sunil compelled me to go and meet Najeeb. He insisted that I should talk to him. Hear him out. And, if possible, write about him. Sunil said that Najeeb's story would be a moral for those who give up and collapse on facing the slightest obstacle. So I went and met Najeeb, a very simple man.

Najeeb was at first reluctant to talk about his experience. 'Those things happened long ago. I have already forgotten about them,' he said. But then, when I urged him to tell me his story, bit by bit he began to narrate the story of that period of his life. One by one, the incidents that he seemed to have forgotten became vivid in front of his eyes. His forceful narrative really surprised me.

After that I met Najeeb many more times and we talked for hours. I questioned him and learned about the minute details of his life in the Gulf. I realized how most of the previous accounts I had heard of that life were vague, superficial and far from reality.

When I went to meet Najeeb for the first time, I had no intention of creating a novel out of his story. I was only curious to know a man who had been through so much in life. But as I learned more about his experience, I couldn't fight the urge to write about it. How many millions of Malayalis live in the Gulf? How many millions have lived and returned to the homeland! But how many of them have really experienced the severity of the desert? I didn't sugarcoat Najeeb's story or fluff it up to please the reader. Even without that, Najeeb's story deserves to be read. This is not just Najeeb's story, it is real life. A goat's life.